Sharon

by

Annette F. Wilcox

En Route Books and Media, LLC

Saint Louis, MO

ENROUTE
Make the time

En Route Books and Media, LLC

5705 Rhodes Avenue

St. Louis, MO 63109

Contact us at **contact@enroutebooksandmedia.com**

Cover Credit: Sebastian Mahfood using ChatGPT and a photo of the Cathedral of the Madeleine, Salt Lake City, Utah, used with permission of the Very Reverend Martin Diaz, Rector.

Copyright 2025 Annette F. Wilcox

ISBN-13: 979-8-88870-327-4

Library of Congress Control Number:

Available online at https://catalog.loc.gov

For the real Sharon (and the real Snickers),
with fond memories

Table of Contents

[This story is set in Salt Lake City, Utah in the late 1990's,
just before the proliferation of cell phones, social media,
and "screen time."]

Chapter 1

The Meeting

It was late afternoon in Salt Lake City on the first cold day of October—the first real autumn-like weather, air cool and crisp. The neighborhood's houses were modest—each with a small yard and a few trees. Some had hedges. Mrs. Harris came out of her front gate and shut it behind her, then walked briskly down the street on her way to the nearby grocery store. She had decided to make brownies, and she needed eggs.

As she walked past the house next door, its side door opened and a small figure hurtled out of it, sprinted across the unfenced yard and cannoned into Mrs. Harris, not quite knocking her down. She took a step back and clutched the child, fighting to keep her balance, then looked down into the terror-stricken face of a little girl. Clearly, the child was in a blind panic, shaking with fear.

Mrs. Harris spoke to the fear. "It's okay. I'm here," she said. "You're safe."

The house next door had been unoccupied for quite a while until two days before when a mother and her daughter had moved in. Mrs. Harris had caught glimpses of them but hadn't met either of them until now.

Tears ran down the girl's cheeks, and she still seemed near panic as she stepped back from Mrs. Harris's embrace and they looked at each other.

Mrs. Harris saw a white-faced little girl of eight or nine, dressed in brightly patterned leggings which hung a little loosely on her matchstick legs. An oversized sweater was on her top half. Her hair was escaping wildly from a blonde ponytail. She was still shaking.

The little girl saw, through her tears, an aging woman, plump (or solid?) in a denim jumper and "sensible" shoes, carrying a purse and a tote bag and wearing a neat wool cardigan which almost looked as though it had been ironed. She had gray hair cut short, but curly from a perm, and she was wearing glasses which didn't add anything to her appearance, unless perhaps by giving her the look of a librarian.

"What is it?" asked Mrs. Harris.

"Oh, please!" said the girl. "I heard a noise!"

"Are you alone in the house?"

The girl nodded. "I'm suh-scared," she said. "There isn't supposed to be anyone else there."

"There probably isn't," reassured Mrs. Harris. "Why are you there all alone? Aren't you a bit young?"

"My daddy's sick, and he has to stay in the hospital, and Mama said I'm old enough to wait for her after school, now that I've turned nine. But I'm not!" The last words rose to a wail.

"What time is your mother coming home?" asked Mrs. Harris.

"She said 5:30."

"My goodness, child, it's twenty after five right now. Why don't we just go shut the door to your house, so all the heat doesn't get out, then we can sit right here on the front steps and wait for your mother. Don't worry." Mrs. Harris patted the child's thin back as she spoke. "You don't need to be scared. I won't leave you until your mother comes home."

She reached into her purse for a Kleenex. "Here, wipe your eyes, blow your nose, and calm down. I'll be right back." She started for the side door, to close it.

A small hand slipped into hers, and the girl said, "No, I'll come, too." She had stopped crying, all but a few hiccups and a shuddery breath or two. "You said you wouldn't leave me."

"That's right," agreed Mrs. Harris. She smiled at the girl. "What's your name?"

"I'm Sharon."

"Well, I'm Mrs. Harris. I live next door. I saw you and your mom moving in a few days ago."

They reached the open side door. After shutting it, Mrs. Harris led Sharon back toward the front of the house. She looked down at her and smiled again. This time Sharon smiled back, a watery sort of smile, but definitely a smile. They sat down on a front step of the house.

"Cold, isn't it?" asked Mrs. Harris. "Well, now, your mom will probably be home any minute, but why don't you tell me all about it until she comes. Tell me again how come you were in the house all alone?"

"See, we had to move 'cause Daddy's sick," explained Sharon, pressing up against Mrs. Harris's side for warmth. "I was lucky 'cause I get to go to my same school, but Mama said with only one income she can't afford to pay for after-school care any more, same as we had to move to this house 'cause it's cheaper."

Mrs. Harris nodded her understanding.

"So, Mama said I'm big enough to stay alone for an hour and a half until she gets home from work. I had my birthday last week and I'm nine now, but"—a long tremulous sigh—"I don't think I am."

"What's the matter with your daddy?"

"I don't know. They won't tell me anything. I just hear them whispering. He's been sick for a long time, and now he's in the hospital. I didn't used to always be so scared, not before Daddy got sick. Say, why are we sitting out here? It's cold."

"Well, honey, your mom'll be really worried if she comes home and doesn't find you here. That means I'd better not take you to my house because then she won't know where you are. And your mom doesn't know me, so she might not be too happy if she comes home and finds a strange woman in her house. It's not that cold. Here, sit on my tote bag. It'll keep the cold off your seat."

Sharon stood up, then sat back down on the tote bag which Mrs. Harris laid on the step. Before she did so she asked, "I won't squish anything, will I?"

"No, there's only a book inside. I always carry a book or two because you never know. If I get stuck and have to wait somewhere, I don't mind as long as I've got a book along to read."

"Do you like reading, too? I love reading," announced Sharon.

"Really? What books do you like?" asked Mrs. Harris.

"I like the Baby-Sitter's Club books and *The Magic School Bus,* and when I was little I liked Peter Rabbit only I felt bad for Peter, and I used to like Corduroy, you know, the bear that gets a pocket?"

"Yes, I know. I've got four children. Can you imagine that? They're all grown up now, but they liked Peter Rabbit and Corduroy, too, when they were younger. Did you know there's a book that comes after Peter Rabbit?"

"No way! Is there? With Peter in it?"

"Yes, he's in it, and so is his cousin. It's called *The Tale of Benjamin Bunny*, Benjamin being the cousin's name, and it's about how they go back to Mr. McGregor's garden the next day to try to find Peter's clothes that got made into a scarecrow. I've got the book. I've got quite a few of the good old children's books."

"Oh, I want to read it!" exclaimed Sharon. Cars had been going by from time to time on the mostly quiet street, but now a car slowed as it approached, then turned into the narrow driveway and stopped alongside the house.

Sharon jumped up and ran to the driver's side door. It opened and a pretty, blonde woman with a wistful expression stepped out, looking tired from her long day, only to find herself being hugged by her daughter, who was like a miniature replica of herself.

"Mama, Mama!" cried out Sharon. "I got scared, and I ran outside, and I met our neighbor, and this is her!" dragging her mother by the hand over to the front steps, where Mrs. Harris had just stood up.

The two women introduced themselves: Wilma Harris and Claudine Stover. Mrs. Harris welcomed Sharon's mother to the neighborhood and apologized for not coming over before to introduce herself.

Sharon's mother said, "No problem. I know we're all so busy these days. I haven't even been here much yet, what with one thing and another. What's all this Sharon's telling me?"

"Well, she got scared, I guess, came shooting out of the door like something was after her as I was walking by on my way to the store, so I calmed her down and sat with her for a few minutes, just until you got home. We had a nice discussion about books."

"Oh, thank you so much!" Mrs. Stover looked troubled. "It's such a problem knowing what to do. I really can't afford after-school care right now, and I thought a big girl, nine years old, could stay here by herself for an hour and a half a day, but I don't know ... not if things like this are going to happen."

Nine didn't sound all that big to Mrs. Harris. She watched sympathetically as Sharon hung her head and scraped the toe of her sneaker back and forth on the concrete area in front of the steps.

"I'm sorry, Mama," Sharon quavered. "I just ... I just don't think I can. I hear noises and stuff."

Mrs. Harris looked down at the girl and felt sorry. "Now, would it help if Sharon stayed with me after school? What is it, from 4:00 to 5:30 every day?"

"Oh, we couldn't!" exclaimed Mrs. Stover. "We couldn't put you to that kind of trouble. We don't even know you, and I really couldn't afford to pay much."

"Who said anything about paying? It's true that you don't know me, but if you call one of the priests at the Cathedral downtown, the Catholic one, you know? they'll tell you that I'm okay. Just ask for either of the priests. I'm not working this year, and my time isn't all that valuable. As I was telling Sharon, I raised four children of my own, all grown now, and one of my favorite things is reading to children."

She smiled at Sharon. "I *didn't* tell you that, did I?"

Mrs. Stover was still shaking her head, but she was beginning to look hopeful, too. "But I couldn't ask you to commit your time like that…"

Mrs. Harris jumped in, "If Sharon would like to come, I'd enjoy sharing some books with her. The only thing is there's no TV, so if she wants to watch television it wouldn't work. I could give her a snack, then we could read for a while, maybe play a game. I'd enjoy it if Sharon would like to come."

Sharon was beginning to bounce up and down in place on the driveway, her eyes shining. "Oh, Mama, please let me!" she cried. "She's got the book that comes after Peter Rabbit, did you know that? Oh, Mama, please!"

Sharon's mother pulled the little girl to her side and said, "Well, I'll certainly think about it. I'm sure Sharon would love it"—at which Sharon nodded her head vigorously—"but it seems so much to ask."

"Now, don't you worry about that. You be sure to call the Cathedral. Let me give you my phone number." She jotted a couple of numbers down on a page of the small spiral notebook that she pulled out of her purse, then ripped the sheet out and gave it to Mrs. Stover. "I've given you my number, and I think this is the number of the church. It's in the phone book anyway, under Cathedral of the Madeleine. Either of the priests will give you a good report about me, and then I'll hope to see Sharon tomorrow after school. Please call me and let me know what you decide."

She got ready to leave. "I'd better go to the grocery store before it gets any later. It's nice to meet you both. Now, don't you worry," to Sharon's mother, "and Sharon, if you can come tomorrow, we'll read about Benjamin Bunny."

Mrs. Harris bustled off down the street leaving Sharon and her mother still standing side by side in front of their house.

"I like her, Mama, don't you?" asked Sharon. "She makes me feel safe. Isn't she nice?"

"Yes, Sharon, I like her, too," replied her mother. "I'll call the church in the morning, just to be sure, but I can't imagine there'll be a problem. It sure is nice of her, though."

"Oh, goody!" Sharon began to jump up and down again, and bunny-hopped up the steps to the house.

Chapter 2

Snickers

The next day, a priest having vouched for Mrs. Harris, Sharon's mother called in the middle of the morning to say that she would be grateful to have Mrs. Harris watch Sharon and that she had called the school with a message for Sharon to that effect. Just on this first day Mrs. Harris was out front at four o'clock, standing at the gate of her fenced yard, watching for Sharon, to make sure that she got there safely. Sharon arrived in tears, shaking like a leaf, in much the same condition as the day before. Mrs. Harris led her through the front gate toward the house.

Then things went from bad to worse. Snickers, Mrs. Harris's little white poodle, met them at the front door, barking loudly. Sharon froze, panic-stricken, then shrieked and tried to climb onto Mrs. Harris's head, as though Mrs. Harris were a tree or a barber pole.

Mrs. Harris, handicapped by having a child clinging to her, with hands across her eyes or mouth as Sharon clutched at her, trying to get a better grip and move higher, nearly deafened by Sharon's cries and the dog's barks, nevertheless was able to snag Snickers with a foot. In a stentorian voice, she bellowed, "Snickers, OUT!" then assisted him with her foot, scooping him up and giving him a jump-start down the front steps. She shut the door, managed to pry Sharon loose so she could carry her in a more conventional manner, then took her to a rocking chair in a corner of the living room and rocked

for a while, hugging the child close and patting her on the back, waiting for Sharon's sobs to stop.

After a bit, Sharon was able to sit up and take notice of things
again. Mrs. Harris said, "Now, let's talk about what happened. Snickers took you by surprise, didn't he?"

Sharon nodded.

"And I didn't know you were scared of dogs, or I'd have gotten
him out of the way. It's pretty bad, isn't it?"

Sharon nodded again.

"Were you ever bitten by a dog?"

This time the answer was a shake of the head, no.

"Well, then, what scares you? Talk to me, please."

"I just … it's just…" Sharon found that she hadn't quite stopped
crying. Mrs. Harris patted her on the back some more and resumed
rocking.

After a short interval, Sharon tried again. "I just get scared when
I see one, and then … and then they always bark at me … and …
and … I'm scared they *might* bite."

"I see," said Mrs. Harris consideringly. "Dogs always know if
you're scared—they can smell it or something. And some dogs *are*
dangerous, of course. There are dogs you need to be scared of, especially if they're out on the sidewalk in front of a house; dogs never
can learn that the sidewalk doesn't belong to the house.

"But, *however*," she continued, "Snickers is a very friendly little
dog, and he likes children. He used to belong to my second daughter
more than to any of the rest of us, so little girls are his favorite, really."

Sharon looked up at her doubtfully.

"No, it's true," said Mrs. Harris, answering the look. "It's just that he's a little dog and they tend to be hysterical and bark a lot—though he's smart enough in other ways. But you were already frightened even before Snickers started barking, weren't you?"

Through some new tears, Sharon explained that walking home from school frightened her. She couldn't really explain, though, what she was frightened of, or rather, she was frightened of so many things. She had just learned the way home from school to the new house. She might get lost. A dog might bite her. Big kids might be mean. A stranger might try to kidnap her. She might get hit by a car. In short, something bad might happen. The fact that nothing bad *had* happened didn't seem to reassure her.

Mrs. Harris tried to understand, to put herself in the child's shoes, as it were. She was deeply concerned by the two episodes of panic that she had witnessed in less than twenty-four hours. Sharon's fears seemed to go far beyond anything normal. Even now the little girl was still shaking.

The likeliest thing seemed to her that the world had become a scary place for Sharon because her father was so sick. She had said that she hadn't always been so scared. How could she feel safe with her father in the hospital? It was her father whom she had counted on to keep her safe.

Of course, it wasn't really any use to try to tell Sharon that probably nothing bad would happen on any given day, although that was so. It was undeniably true that bad things did happen sometimes. Sharon's fears weren't completely unrealistic. Children did sometimes get lost, bitten by dogs, teased by older children, even hit by cars or kidnapped by strangers. The fact that these things rarely happen, and could often be prevented by being careful, was not a help to Sharon.

What Sharon probably didn't know, and certainly couldn't say, was that her feelings of anxiety were at the root of the matter. She tried to explain her feelings by talking about what might happen, but the feeling of impending doom was really much more general and came before the fears, or so it seemed to Mrs. Harris.

She thought quickly about the possibilities for helping, not wanting to promise a thing unless she knew for sure that she could do it. A promise to a child needed to be fulfilled, in Mrs. Harris's opinion. But having thought it through, she asked Sharon, "Would it help if I were to meet you at your school when you get out and walk home with you?"

Sharon's eyes widened in surprise, but joy and relief lit her face, too. "Would you?" she asked in an uncertain voice, then sniffed.

"Yes, I think so. Maybe not quite every day, but most days I could. I'll just make it into Snickers's afternoon walk. Probably do me good to get a bit more exercise anyway."

"Oh, that would be better than anything!" Sharon exclaimed, forgetting her tears, but still a bit shaky. "I wouldn't be scared at all if *you* were there."

Mrs. Harris smiled at the strong feeling with which the words were uttered. "We'll start tomorrow," she promised, in a matter-of-fact tone of voice. "I'll do it as long as you need me to. You may find after a while that you're fine on your own. Let's give it a try."

Sharon didn't try to hide her jubilation. "That will be so good!" she said. "Mama takes me in the morning, so that will fix *everything*."

Mrs. Harris looked at Sharon thoughtfully. There was something endearing about the girl. She had bright eyes and an intelligent little face.

Once all this was settled, Sharon began to look around her, taking an interest in Mrs. Harris and her house. Today, Mrs. Harris was dressed in jeans, a Fair Isle sweater with a pattern of whales around the yoke, and Birkenstock sandals through which could be seen thick woolen socks. Sharon thought she looked old, but comfortable. She especially liked the whales, which alternated blue and purple around the yoke of the sweater.

The house itself was a surprise to Sharon. She was used to white walls, with a few pictures hung here and there, or perhaps a mirror, like the places she had always lived. This living room was like nothing she had ever seen. There were books everywhere! Every wall had a bookcase or two, all of them loaded with books.

Mrs. Harris caught the look on her face and laughed. "Looks like a library, doesn't it?" she asked. Sharon climbed off Mrs. Harris's lap and turned slowly around, taking it all in. Every bit of wall space not taken up by bookcases was covered with pictures, most of them religious. There was a little ceramic dish with water in it mounted on the wall by the front door. There were needlepointed pictures with religious texts worked into them, pictures of the Virgin Mary and baby Jesus, some small statues even, of men or women wearing long brown or black robes and holding various things. One of the pictures sat on a shelf and had a candle in front of it in a bright blue glass holder. There was a large crucifix hanging on the wall in one corner of the room.

Sharon had never seen, never dreamed of, a room like this. She had never seen religious pictures and didn't know what they represented. That man didn't look happy, pinned up on a cross like that. And what was the water by the door for?

But the room was made cheerful by a fire crackling in the fireplace, and the books intrigued Sharon. Quite a few of them, maybe even half, were children's books. Sharon headed for them, her eyes shining.

"Now you just make yourself at home, dear, and look at anything you want to," said Mrs. Harris. "But come to the kitchen first. I'm going to get us a snack. Are you hungry?"

Sharon nodded. They walked down a hallway to the kitchen. It was clean and bright but just looked like a normal kitchen. There was half a shelf of cookbooks, but otherwise the room was devoid of books.

"I thought we'd have the brownies that I made last night," said Mrs. Harris. "Do you like brownies?"

Sharon laughed. "Everybody likes brownies, don't they?"

"Almost everyone, I would think. What would you like to drink: milk or water?"

"Milk, please."

They heard a scratching at the back door, which opened off the kitchen. Sharon looked up quickly at Mrs. Harris. Snickers had apparently made his way around to the back of the house.

Mrs. Harris said, "Ah … he's asking in." She looked at Sharon and Sharon looked back at her.

"Would you be willing to make friends with him? I love him very much, you know, and I'd like to see you two be friends."

Sharon hesitated. "Wouldn't he maybe bite me?" she asked. "'Cause he'd know I'm scared?"

"Snickers? He might bite, I suppose, if you stepped on him or pulled his ears or tail. But you're too old for that kind of thing, aren't you? He would never bite otherwise. Never! Let me introduce him to you carefully. Just sit down on that chair over there"—pointing to a chair by the kitchen table—"and don't worry. Snickers likes children, and he'll be happy to meet you. The main danger is that he might be a little too happy and start licking you or jumping up on you. He'll probably bark a little, too, but I'll tell him to be quiet."

The scratching was becoming insistent.

Sharon sat down, watching in some trepidation as Mrs. Harris opened the back door. She clenched her teeth and braced herself but managed not to cry out.

A small whirlwind of a dog rushed in and dashed over to Sharon, barking. Mrs. Harris picked Snickers up and patted him, at which he gave her chin a quick, absentminded lick, then resumed his looking at Sharon from Mrs. Harris's arms. But he had stopped barking.

Mrs. Harris said, "Now, Sharon, this is Snickers. Snickers, this is Sharon. You be good," she added, patting the dog and giving him a hug. Then she spoke to Sharon again, "I'm going to put him down again, and he'll come up to you. Can you hold your hand out, palm down?" She held out her own hand in illustration. "He'll sniff the back of your hand and then he'll always know it's you from now on. Are you ready?"

Sharon took a deep breath and nodded, still apprehensive. Though, really, it was hard to be horribly frightened of such a small dog.

Mrs. Harris leaned over to put Snickers down, but he forestalled her by jumping out of her arms when he was still a couple of feet from the floor. He trotted over to Sharon, who had obediently put her hand out. He gave it a couple of long sniffs, then a quick lick.

"That's his way of saying hello," remarked Mrs. Harris. "You can pat him now if you'd like."

Sharon reached out and felt the dog's curly white fur. He gave her wrist a lick, then trotted over to his water bowl and began to lap.

"What do you think?" asked Mrs. Harris. "Are you doing all right?"

Sharon nodded. "He's really cute, actually. It's just that he moves so fast sometimes."

"That's true," allowed Mrs. Harris. "Would you like to be his friend for life?" She was teasing now, as Sharon could see from the way she smiled and lifted one eyebrow.

"What do you mean?" Sharon answered the tease with a shaky smile.

"Just give him a dog biscuit," Mrs. Harris explained, as she reached up into a cabinet above the kitchen counter and took a small, bone-shaped biscuit out of a box. To Sharon it made only the smallest of small sounds, but Snickers could hear the sound of a dog biscuit being taken out of the box from anywhere in the house. He capered over to Mrs. Harris and began dancing around in front of her, waiting joyfully, but impatiently, for the treat.

Before she handed the biscuit to the girl Mrs. Harris explained, "He's wants this, so he'll come over and put his paw on your knee probably, trying to reach for it. But don't you give it to him. He has to be sitting to get a dog biscuit. Just say, 'Snickers, sit!' and hold up your first finger." She demonstrated as she spoke. Sharon noticed that Snickers sat down, but only momentarily. "Then wait until he sits and hold out the biscuit. He should take it gently, not snatch it."

It happened exactly as she said. Snickers watched the transfer of the dog biscuit, danced over to where Sharon was sitting, found her so low to the ground that he put his paw on her knee and stretched up, reaching for the coveted biscuit. Sharon held her right hand, the one with the biscuit in it, high up out of his reach. With her left hand she pointed her first finger while she said, "Snickers, sit!"

Instantly, the dog sank back on his haunches and watched eagerly as the dog biscuit descended toward him. When it was low enough, he opened his mouth and took it gently, delicately even, from Sharon's hand. Then he walked over to where the hall carpeting met the tile of the kitchen floor, turned around until he was facing them, and lay down flat on his stomach, his short little hind legs sticking straight out behind him into the hallway, to eat the biscuit. Sharon had never seen anything like the way he used his paws, holding the biscuit straight up and down by bracing one paw on either side of it, then turning his head sideways to bite the top of it off.

Mrs. Harris continued getting the humans' snack, putting the pan of brownies on the table and pouring Sharon a glass of milk. Then she sat down at the table with her cup of tea and helped Sharon to a brownie.

"What kind of dog is he?" Sharon wondered, watching Snickers eat.

"Oh, he's a poodle. I've never been sure what size of poodle," answered Mrs. Harris. "I know he doesn't look much like one right

now because he really needs grooming. He'll look completely different when I bring him back from his appointment with the groomer
tomorrow."

"What do you mean, what size of poodle?" asked Sharon. "Are
there different sizes?"

"Yes, several. Some poodles are really big." She held her hand
out at about waist level. "Those are called standard poodles. Snickers
is either a miniature or a toy poodle. He only weighs eleven or twelve
pounds. I've had him for years, and I'm very fond of him, but he's a
funny dog. Poodles are, you know. He has his little ways, like the way
he eats a biscuit. And he's scared of brooms. I got him from the Den-
ver Dumb Friends League when he about was six months old, and
he's always been frightened of brooms since I've had him."

Snickers seemed to know that he was being talked about. He had
raised his head from the dog biscuit and was watching Mrs. Harris.
His brown eyes were bright.

"When I first got him, he'd start to yelp and run away if I so
much as picked up a broom," Mrs. Harris continued. "That was
years ago. He doesn't mind them so much now, doesn't yelp or run,
but he still won't stay in the room if I have a broom. He just leaves
promptly and quietly. I figure someone hit him with a broom when
he was a puppy. He wasn't absolutely perfectly housebroken when I
got him; maybe he got punished for that—or maybe a broom just
fell on him once. We'll never know."

"How old is he?" asked Sharon.

"Older than you, dear. He's ten. Didn't you say you just turned
nine?"

"Yeah. My birthday was last week."

"Well, Snickers is ten," Mrs. Harris repeated.

After the snack, they moved back to the living room. Mrs. Harris found *The Tale of Benjamin Bunny* and called Sharon to sit beside her on the sofa so she could see the pictures as Mrs. Harris read. Snickers came, too, and curled up on Mrs. Harris's other side, having been forcibly prevented from sitting on her lap. Sharon listened to the story. Mrs. Harris read well, with a low, attractive voice, and made the story come alive to Sharon.

After the book, which horrified Sharon when Benjamin Bunny's father whipped both little bunnies, Sharon climbed down off the sofa and went to renew her acquaintance with some of the picture books on the bottom shelves of the bookcases. There were also quite a few older picture books that she had never seen before. She lay on the sheepskin rug in front of the fireplace, a whole pile of books by her side, and looked through them one by one.

Before she knew it, it was 5:30. Sharon's mom telephoned to say she was home, and Mrs. Harris watched Sharon safely across the yard to the house next door.

Chapter 3

Early Days

The next day set the pattern for the many days that followed. Mrs. Harris put a jacket on just after 3 o'clock then, taking with her a delighted little dog, dressed in one of the sweaters he loved to wear, she started the walk to school. It was about a twenty-minute walk each way, so she allowed plenty of time to be there for the 3:30 dismissal.

Arriving early at the long, low brick building, she found quite a few other women waiting for school to get out. She passed the time chatting with a couple of the mothers and fielding comments about Snickers, who was always glad of any extra attention.

The appointment with the groomer had left him looking very tidy, though shorn. The bright red bows the groomer had put on his ears hadn't even come off yet—they never lasted more than a day—and he had the immediately-after-grooming look that Mrs. Harris didn't much like. He looked strange she thought, when his muzzle had just been shaved, almost like a different dog. It always took her a week or so to get used to how narrow his nose looked, like a greyhound's, and by the time she did get used to it the hair was growing out again anyway. But he undeniably looked like a poodle and other people often admired him when he was so freshly groomed. She did like the look of his paws. The groomer was always asked to give him what is called "clean" paws, and they reminded Mrs. Harris of little monkey hands somehow.

Snickers was so busy being the center of attention, and Mrs. Harris was so involved in talking with the other women, that at first they hardly noticed as a bell rang and children began coming out of the main door of the school—first a trickle, then a flood of children from grades one to six.

It was Sharon who spotted Mrs. Harris and Snickers, standing inside a circle of admiring children who stretched out their hands to the little dog and called to him, hoping he would let them pat him. "Oh, isn't he a darling?" "Look how cute he is in his little sweater."

"Doesn't he mind wearing it?" asked one of the mothers.

"No, he really likes wearing clothes," laughed Mrs. Harris. "What he minds is when I take it off. He seems to feel the cold more when he's just been groomed, like today. When I hold a sweater out, he runs over and tries to stick his head in it."

The other women laughed. Sharon pulled at Mrs. Harris's sleeve. She said good-bye to the group, and they started for home, Sharon walking happily at Mrs. Harris's side.

They talked about Sharon's day: the geography test, music class, what the teacher was like, and arrived back at Mrs. Harris's house invigorated and red-cheeked, ready for a snack. Snickers, too, got his usual dog biscuit, which he ate in his usual way, biting the top off and working his way down it.

Mrs. Harris became a familiar sight at the grade school over the next weeks, and Snickers didn't draw as much attention after the first few days, but he gained a few friends who always looked for him and gave him a pat.

That was a partial solution to some of Sharon's fears, but Mrs. Harris often noticed how on edge the child seemed to be. She was alert to every sound and jumped a little at any unexpected noise. The only way Mrs. Harris could think of to help was by reading Sharon books about children who had overcome fears and adversity. She began to give some careful consideration to which books she was going to read to Sharon.

The pattern of their afternoon time together was to walk home from school, arriving just before four o'clock, eat a snack and talk until about four-thirty, then read for forty-five minutes to an hour. The time passed very quickly. An hour and a half didn't seem like much time at all, and they had to be careful not to talk too long and get their reading time cut into.

Mrs. Harris didn't see much of Sharon's mother. Mrs. Stover always telephoned when she got home from work, then Mrs. Harris would watch Sharon safely through the front gate, over to her own yard and into the house next door, but she rarely caught even a glimpse of Sharon's mother. One Saturday morning, though, Mrs. Harris saw Claudine Stover outside without Sharon. She had been watching for such an opportunity and went over to talk about Sharon's fearfulness.

She found that Mrs. Stover was worried, too, but didn't understand why Sharon was so fearful any more than Mrs. Harris did. Mrs. Stover had, of course, heard from Sharon about how frightened she had been the first day that she walked to Mrs. Harris's house, and how Mrs. Harris was now picking her up from school every day. She apologized for the trouble her daughter was causing Mrs. Harris and confirmed Sharon's story that she hadn't always been so fearful, though "she was always a cautious one" as Mrs. Stover put it. But it

had definitely gotten worse in the year-and-a-half of the father's illness.

They talked about how to help Sharon but didn't come to any
very definite conclusions, holding the idea of a counselor in reserve
as perhaps unnecessary and certainly unaffordable. One positive as-
pect to the situation was that Sharon seemed happy at school. Mrs.
Harris thought it was a real accomplishment that her mother had
managed to move houses without changing Sharon's school, thus
saving the child one transition at least.

The books they read! It's surprising how many books you can
get through by reading five days a week for several months. They
started with *The Boxcar Children*. Sharon had missed it somehow.
But she liked the story, especially the all-black pictures, almost like
silhouettes, and Benny's little pink cup. Then they read *Matilda and
Her Family*, a story of a mother cat and her kittens, and what happens to each kitten as it grows up.

Next came *Trina Finds a Brother*, translated from the Norwegian, a story about a little Norwegian girl who lives on a freighter
with her mother and sea captain father, and sails all over the world.
When they visit North Africa, Trina and her mother find a little boy
living on the street in a big box, a boy who eventually becomes
Trina's adopted brother.

These were the earliest chapter books and were the books that
Mrs. Harris always started with for children who were beyond the
age of picture books. After them, she began her plan of trying to
make the books she read illustrative of children who had faced and
overcome fears.

The first of these fear books was *Understood Betsy*, by Dorothy Canfield, the story of a very timid orphan girl who has been raised by her anxiety-ridden Aunt Frances, a relative from her mother's side of the family, but who at the age of nine is sent to live with a different set of relatives, these ones from her father's side of the family. The new relatives are much more experienced at raising children. During the course of the book, Elizabeth Ann, as she's called by the first set of relatives, or Betsy, as she's called by the second set, gradually becomes a much happier and more courageous little girl, facing and overcoming obstacles as she's guided by the new relatives.

Sharon was interested in Betsy.

"She's sort of like me, isn't she?" she asked Mrs. Harris one afternoon as they had finished a chapter and were sitting on the sofa considering whether or not to start another.

"Yes, I suppose she is in some ways," agreed Mrs. Harris.

"What do you think makes some children scared, like me and Betsy?" pursued Sharon.

"Well," answered Mrs. Harris, "part of Betsy's problem was that her Aunt Frances was scared of a lot of things, too, don't you think?"

"Yes, that's true," Sharon nodded.

"I think children need to have strong adults behind them," suggested Mrs. Harris. "That can give them a sense of security."

Sharon thought this over. "Like Cousin Ann and Aunt Abigail seem all, sort of, calm compared with Aunt Frances?" she asked tentatively. "Nothing Betsy ever does gets them upset."

"Right," nodded Mrs. Harris.

"Um-hmm," said Sharon, thinking this over. "But my parents aren't like Aunt Frances."

"No," allowed Mrs. Harris. "And I don't think you're just like Betsy. She was scared of school and tests, wasn't she? You worry about other things, things that could happen but hardly ever do. It's kind of like you're ruining your life for things that you will probably never have to face. Or if you did have to face them you could probably cope just fine."

"But it isn't something that I *do*," protested Sharon. "It doesn't feel that way, anyway. It's more like what I *am*, or at least it's how I feel."

Mrs. Harris nodded. "That's why I haven't brought the subject up. Because I don't think talking about it really helps. Probably it will get better if you start feeling more secure. You're worried about your dad, aren't you?"

"Yeah, I really am," admitted Sharon.

"A lot of children are older than you are before they have to realize that bad things can happen in this world," Mrs. Harris said. "Of course, some learn it even earlier than you."

"Is there an answer?" asked Sharon. "I mean, something that would make me less scared?"

"Your dad might get better," Mrs. Harris seemed almost to ask this rather than state it.

"Yeah, I don't know," sighed Sharon. "But I'm not even sure that would help because now I know it's possible he could die. I mean, he could even die some other way, couldn't he? When before I never thought of it. I just thought he'd always be there."

"Well, the real answer is to find your security in God," stated Mrs. Harris. "Knowing that God loves you and will always help."

"Is that it?" asked Sharon, looking at Mrs. Harris in a puzzled way. "Is that what makes you so safe and secure? I always feel better when I'm with you, and I've wondered a lot why."

"Maybe that *is* why," agreed Mrs. Harris. "I'm glad I have that effect on you anyway."

"I don't know anything about God," said Sharon sadly. "I'm not even sure I believe in Him."

"Maybe we need to do something about that," answered Mrs. Harris.

Sharon loved the next book, *Miss Happiness and Miss Flower* by Rumer Godden, the story of an unhappy girl who has been sent home from India to live with her aunt, uncle, and cousins in England. Nona, too, is afraid almost constantly, but gradually overcomes her fears of the new living situation by helping two little Japanese dolls, sent by a great-aunt, to "feel at home." Nona learns about Japanese culture, finally persuading one of her cousins to build a Japanese dollhouse for the dolls. There are diagrams and specifications for the dollhouse at the end of the book.

Sharon liked the book a lot, and now she, too, wanted Japanese dolls and to build a dollhouse.

Mrs. Harris sympathized, but explained that the book seemed to affect most people that way, that she herself had wanted those things, too, ever since she first read the book in childhood, but that she had never seen any dolls of the right size and kind, especially any with the "cloth bodies and stuffing" that made them posable. She had long since stopped looking.

"Although if I ever saw any…"

She further explained that reading books often had that effect, making the reader want a horse, or a summer cabin or to be a figure skater, ballet dancer, bareback rider or to live in foster care even, because books could make all those things sound wonderful.

"I wish you could have Japanese dolls, though," she sighed. "I've never known where to find them. And, really, it would be pretty hard to build that dollhouse—either that or you'd have to have lots of money to get someone to build it for you."

Mrs. Harris seemed to know book after book, each a little more interesting than the one before. So, they read *Runaway Girl* by Ruth Morris. In it an orphan girl has been sent from a big city to live with distant relatives in the Outback of Australia. The relatives are so unfriendly that she cuts her hair to look like a boy's and sets off across the Outback, driving a horse and wagon. She is terrified much of the time, of course. Several people are kind to her, including an old cattle herder ("drover" in Australian English) who gives her a puppy. She has various adventures and, by the end of the book, has found a good family to adopt her.

Chapter 4

Sharon's Dad Comes Home

Mrs. Harris became very fond of Sharon during their daily walks home from school and their talks at snack time. Sharon was timid, but at school it apparently didn't show much, as she made herself do what the other fourth graders did and kept her worries about her father to herself.

Mrs. Harris came to realize that Sharon was an excellent student. It was unusual for her to get less than 95% on any test or worksheet, whether spelling, arithmetic, social studies, or any other subject. Nor did Sharon care how hard she had to work to do well. In school, apparently, Sharon thought only about schoolwork and perhaps even found school to be a refuge from her home troubles—in much the same way that she was coming to view her time at Mrs. Harris's house.

Troubles at home were several. Because of her father's illness, there was a lack of money. Luckily Sharon's father was a veteran which meant that medical care wasn't so much of an expense, and he had very good insurance from work, but of course he wasn't able to work, hadn't been able to work for months. Sharon's mother was trying to support Sharon and herself on a secretary's salary. She was carrying a heavy burden, trying to work full-time and spend time with her husband, in addition to bringing up a little girl and doing the housework, cooking, and laundry. It was these last three that were usually neglected, Mrs. Harris learned. Sharon and her mother

were living in less-than-ideal circumstances. Meals were impro-
vised. The house had never gotten completely uncluttered from the
move. Clean clothes were sometimes lacking.

Mrs. Stover visited Sharon's father on her lunch hour every day
and talked with him on the phone every night. On weekends she
took Sharon to the hospital with her, but Sharon only went in to see
her father briefly each time, then sat on a bench in the hallway while
her parents visited together.

Sharon's father looked different these days. For one thing, he had
lost all his hair. And he looked thin. It almost seemed to Sharon as
though a scary stranger was taking her father's place. So, she was
happier sitting out in the hall, or lying on one of the benches if there
weren't too many people around.

Mrs. Harris decided early on to allow Sharon to borrow books.
She found a spare canvas tote bag and advised Sharon to keep borrowed books in it unless she was actually reading them. That way
they would be less likely to "go missing." Sharon began borrowing
stacks of picture books that looked interesting, as well as other books
that Mrs. Harris didn't intend to read aloud to her, such as *Uncle
Arthur's Bedtime Stories*, which Sharon loved—loved for the moral
in each story and for the old-fashioned pictures of happy, healthy,
well-cared-for children.

She took the tote bag with her when she and her mother went to
visit her father at the VA Hospital on weekends. The books helped
to pass the time out in the hallway, which didn't seem so long to her
anymore.

After she had exhausted Mrs. Harris's collection of picture books, she began to borrow old *Reader's Digests* along with one chapter book at a time. Mrs Harris had quite a few shelves of *Reader's Digests* out in her garage and didn't mind how many Sharon took. Sharon loved the jokes, although she didn't always understand them. She occasionally read a story or article, too, as her interest was caught. And she looked at the old ads for cars and appliances that now looked so out-of-date but presumably had looked new and modern back then.

Her father's illness bothered Sharon a lot, but she didn't exactly know what to do with her botheration. Her mother didn't seem to want to talk about it. The few times Sharon tried to bring it up, her mother put on an artificial smile which hurt Sharon to look at, and though tears were shining behind her eyes, told Sharon that Daddy would be well soon.

Sharon knew better than that, could feel instinctively that her mother didn't believe it, but didn't know how to break through the barrier of that bright smile. She lay awake at night quite often, wondering about death, and sometimes cried herself to sleep. She didn't know much about death. Of course, she had seen dead birds from time to time and once a dead kitten. She couldn't imagine her father being dead, though. Maybe she could ask Mrs Harris. But would Mrs Harris know or be able to explain? It would be awful if she put on that same smile that Sharon's mother used.

It might be worth a try, Sharon thought. But she put it off from day to day. She needed to work up the courage to broach the topic. Mrs. Harris *had* helped whenever Sharon was frightened and they had talked about fear more than once, not just when reading *Understood Betsy.*

One day, when they were sitting over their tea (Mrs. Harris) and hot chocolate (Sharon), Mrs. Harris had mentioned casually, "You know, my mother left me alone in the house with my little brothers one time when I was about six. And I got frightened just like you did the day we met."

"You *did*?" asked Sharon, growing a little round-eyed. "Why were *you* scared?"

"Well, as I recall we heard a noise, just like you did. I'm sure now that it was only the house creaking. Houses do creak you know, especially old ones. My mother hadn't wanted the bother of getting us dressed to go out—it must have been winter, I suppose—and left us home 'just for fifteen or twenty minutes' as she said, to go get my father from work. My brothers were four and two if I was six. It's the only time she ever tried that until we were much, much older." Mrs. Harris chuckled reminiscently.

"Why? What did you do? Did you run out of the house like me?"

"No, my mom and dad came home and found the three of us all curled up together under one of the beds. We were so scared that we couldn't even answer when they called our names; we were just paralyzed with fear. They had to look all over the house for us and that scared us even worse, hearing footsteps walking around. I remember my mom peeking under the bed at us when she finally found us and saying something like, 'Well, that's the last time I do *that*!'"

Sharon giggled. "That's funny."

"So, you see, I wasn't all that surprised when you came running out of the house. Wasn't surprised at all, really."

Sharon felt good inside. Mrs. Harris made what she had done sound normal, maybe even inevitable, rather than like the failure Sharon had thought it to be. They had gone to read soon after that and Sharon hadn't thought a lot more about it, but now it made her think that maybe she *could* ask Mrs. Harris about her father and death.

The next week Sharon came out of school one day, hopping with excitement. As they walked home together Sharon was eager to tell Mrs. Harris the reason for her high spirits.

"My daddy's coming home!" she exclaimed joyfully, as she trotted along beside Mrs. Harris and Snickers. "Mama just told me this morning. I've been waiting all day!"

"When is he coming?" asked Mrs. Harris.

"Mama said he'd be there when I got home from school," replied the little girl.

"Well, that's good news. You'll want to go straight home and not read today, I'm sure."

Sharon nodded agreement. "I can't wait to see Daddy. Probably he's getting all better." Her face was lit up with happiness.

Mrs. Harris smiled down at Sharon as she took her mittened hand to cross the one major street between the school and her house.

"I sure hope so," agreed Mrs. Harris. "Some things are more important than reading. You just come back when you can. Do you want me to pick you up at school tomorrow?"

"Yes," declared Sharon. "And we'll read too, won't we? I like reading a lot, but just today it's too exciting."

They separated as they reached Mrs. Harris's house and Sharon ran home.

The next day, Mrs. Harris was grieved to see Sharon's chastened demeanor when she met her in the school yard.

The little girl came dragging out of school, looking woebegone. Even her ponytail seemed to hang down limply. After greeting each other, she and Mrs. Harris walked along in silence for a few minutes, then Mrs. Harris looked down at Sharon and asked, "Want to talk about it?"

Sharon gave her a troubled look and her lower lip began to quiver.

"I held it in all day," she began. "I wanted to cry, but I didn't."

Mrs. Harris nodded, then gave Snickers's leash a yank to get him away from an interesting-smelling piece of trash on the sidewalk.

"Yes, of course. Nobody cries at school if they can help it," she sympathized. "It's your dad?"

"He's awful sick, Mrs. Harris," said Sharon. "He's all… he scares me, he looks so sick. He's so thin and … and kind of white looking. It wasn't so bad seeing him in the hospital, but at home…" Tears began to roll down her cheeks, and Mrs. Harris took her hand, squeezing it for comfort.

"Mom said they gave him some new treatment. I thought since he was coming home he'd look better and get well, but he looks so sick. Now I just don't know," Sharon ended.

Mrs. Harris reached into her jacket pocket for a Kleenex, which she gave the girl.

Sharon managed to stop the tears, at least for the moment. She let go of Mrs. Harris's hand to blow her nose and mop up generally. They walked on, crossing the busy street and nearing Mrs. Harris's house.

"Do you want to read today?" Mrs. Harris asked gently. "Or talk some more?"

Sharon nodded. "Maybe both? I do want to read. I just … even if I didn't like reading so much I'd still want to come 'cause … 'cause I really don't want to go home yet. It scares me seeing him looking so sick," she wound up lamely.

Mrs. Harris looked at her sympathetically. She asked if Sharon's dad was alone in the house and learned that he was, but that a visiting nurse was coming by twice a day to check on him and help him with anything he needed. And Sharon's mother was coming home on her lunch hour.

They turned in at Mrs. Harris's gate and went into the house. Sharon sat down on the kitchen floor and held Snickers in her arms. She hugged him while Mrs. Harris fixed the day's snack.

After they had eaten, they went into the living room. Sharon hugged Snickers again while Mrs. Harris read from the current book.

Chapter 5

Fear

Sharon's dad was home for about two weeks, but one day Mrs. Harris happened to look out her window and saw an ambulance parked in front of the Stover's house, so she wasn't surprised, when Mrs. Stover called, to learn that Sharon's father had been taken back to the hospital.

Sharon hadn't been told anything yet, but Mrs. Stover asked if she could possibly leave Sharon with Mrs. Harris the next day, a Saturday. She wanted to be at the hospital for a procedure that they were planning to do on her husband.

This change in routine caused one more incident of trouble with Snickers. Ever since the first day when Sharon had been so frightened by him it had happened that she had always met the little dog outside at her school when Mrs. Harris came for her in the afternoon. He hadn't barked because he was off his own "turf."

Mrs. Harris planned to take Sharon to the downtown public library. There was a branch library much nearer their neighborhood, but Mrs. Harris usually went to the main library downtown because it had more of the older books that she preferred.

Sharon walked over to Mrs. Harris's house at nine o'clock the next morning, as her mother had arranged, and rang the doorbell. Snickers, as he always did when the doorbell rang, set up a ruckus, barking loudly and running back and forth between the front door and the kitchen where Mrs. Harris was sitting over a second cup of coffee.

By the time Mrs. Harris got to the door, she found that Sharon was too frightened by the barking to come in, and when Snickers dashed up to her, still barking, Sharon turned to run. Mrs. Harris managed to grab Snickers by the collar and, picking him up, carried him to the garage and shut him in, then returned to the frightened child. Sharon had stopped running once Mrs. Harris had Snickers safe and was now working her way back to the front door, but with tears on her face and shaking all over.

"Don't be frightened, dear," said Mrs. Harris, hugging her.

"But he *barked* at me," quavered Sharon, starting to sob again. "I thought we were friends. Why did he bark at me?"

"He always barks when someone comes to the front door. It has nothing to do with who you are or whether or not he knows you. He's just making sure I know you're here," Mrs. Harris explained. "He's excited and it's as though he's saying, 'Sharon's come! She's here! She's here!'"

Sharon smiled through her tears and accepted that; really, she and Snickers were good friends now. He often sat on her lap while she listened to Mrs. Harris read. Even so, any sudden noise continued to make her shake, including Snickers barking for any reason.

She was frightened at the library, too, though not at the children's room where Mrs. Harris took her first. Sharon spent some time picking out a couple of books, then sat on a beanbag chair reading while Mrs. Harris continued to look around at the shelves of children's books.

Wanting to search out some books in adult fiction, Mrs. Harris offered to leave Sharon in the children's room, under the watchful eyes of the nearby children's librarian, but Sharon preferred to come with her. The general part of the library frightened her, though. She held tightly to Mrs. Harris's hand and looked around fearfully at the homeless men sitting at tables, reading or dozing.

Mrs. Harris was of the opinion, along with the librarians, that a child alone was, in fact, not very safe at the downtown library, but of course Sharon was not alone. She looked down at Sharon and asked, "What are you so frightened of? I'm right here with you."

Sharon's grip on her hand got even tighter, but no answer was forthcoming.

"You know," Mrs. Harris remarked casually, "I'd give my life to save you."

Sharon looked up quickly. Mrs Harris met her gaze and smiled. "I won't have to, but I would. Please don't worry so. I can keep you safe here as long as you stay within sight of me."

That helped. Sharon was able to allow Mrs. Harris the use of her hand, though she still kept very close.

When they had left the library and were driving through the late autumn day with its blue sky and, by now, nearly leafless trees, Mrs. Harris looked over at Sharon and said, "I wish I could help you more with this fear thing." Her voice was troubled.

"But you do help," said Sharon, surprised. "I don't know why I feel so safe with you. Usually, I don't even worry at all when I'm with you. But those men in the library were scary."

"Well, old people sometimes are scary to children," Mrs. Harris agreed. "And those men could seem scary even if they were just trying to be friendly." She paused and considered what she had said. "*Especially* if they were trying to be friendly," she corrected herself, and added, "A few of them might even be dangerous. But they know better than to do anything when a grown-up's around."

Sharon nodded.

"They're just there to escape the cold," concluded Mrs. Harris. "Poor guys. If I were homeless, I'd spend a lot of time at the library, too."

As they had so much time on this Saturday, Mrs. Harris suggested stopping at the park on the way home so Sharon could play for a while. She wanted to keep Sharon too busy to worry about whatever procedure her father was undergoing, but she had no idea if she was succeeding or not. Sharon swung on the swings and slid down the slide for a while. Then she came over to where Mrs. Harris was sitting on a park bench, praying a Rosary, and asked if the park had a restroom. It did, of course, and Mrs. Harris walked her over to a small cement block building with metal doors.

Sharon chickened out when they actually got there, though. She couldn't bring herself to go in. Mrs. Harris offered to take her inside, but Sharon refused, saying that she had changed her mind. They went back to the swings, but about ten minutes later Sharon asked again, and again couldn't bring herself to go in. Mrs. Harris wasn't going to offer to go into a toilet stall with a nine-year old but suggested that maybe they should go home right then, and Sharon agreed.

When they got to the car, though, Sharon pulled at Mrs. Harris's sleeve. "Oh, no," she whispered.

Mrs. Harris looked at Sharon and saw a tell-tale puddle on the ground between Sharon's feet, getting bigger as she watched. She at once became brisk.

"Oh, dear," she exclaimed. "Just stand there a second while I get newspapers from the trunk," and came back with some newspapers which she laid on the passenger seat. Giving Sharon a sympathetic pat on the shoulder, she told her to climb in and sit on the newsprint. "It'll save the upholstery," she explained.

She bustled around to the driver's side of the car, climbed in and started the engine. "We'll go straight home and get you cleaned up and dry, then you'll feel better," she reassured Sharon. She looked over at the girl, who was so humiliated that a tear escaped and rolled down her cheek as Mrs. Harris watched.

"Don't make too much of it," she advised Sharon. "It's not the worst thing in the world, and we'll soon have you fixed up."

"It isn't?" Sharon's voice was shaky.

"Well, no, there are lots of worse things. I know it's not what you wanted and that it's very embarrassing for you. Just hang tight. We'll be home in a minute. Your mom hides a key, doesn't she?"

Sharon nodded.

"You know where it is?"

Again, a nod.

"Okay, we'll let ourselves in and get you some clean clothes. You can go in the bathroom and wash up. Then we'll go back to my house and get lunch, okay?"

"Okay," Sharon agreed in a small voice.

Once they had let themselves into the Stover house, Sharon disappeared into her room and came out shortly, carrying a pile consisting of leggings, a pair of socks, and underpants.

Mrs. Harris looked at her feet and asked, "What about your shoes? Did they get wet?"

Sharon moved her feet around in her shoes a little and grimaced, then nodded yes.

"When you're done, I can stuff some newspaper in them and that'll help them dry," said Mrs. Harris. "I hope you have another pair."

"Yeah, I have my new sneakers. These are the old ones."

"Well, that's good. Good thing you wore them today. Not that you knew."

Sharon was behind the bathroom door by now, which was mostly closed.

Mrs Harris spoke through the door. "In the meantime, wet a washcloth with warm water, wring it out until it isn't dripping anymore, then put just a little soap on it and wash yourself, including down both your legs. After that you can rinse the soap out of the washcloth, wring it out again and wipe the soap off your skin before drying off with a towel. Okay? Can you do all that?"

"Uh-huh," answered Sharon.

After a minute or two, Sharon's voice came from behind the bathroom door.

"Why are you being so nice to me? Why aren't you mad?"

"Why, honey, I know you didn't do it on purpose. I'll tell you an embarrassing story about me if you like," Mrs. Harris offered.

"What?" came an interested voice.

"Well," Mrs. Harris cleared her throat, "the last toilet accident that I had I was older than you are now."

"You *were*?"

Sharon opened the door and stared at Mrs. Harris with big eyes. She was dressed in the dry clothes. The wet ones were in a heap on the bathroom floor.

"You stayed dry above the waist, right?" Mrs. Harris asked.

"Right," Sharon answered, but she was preoccupied with the story Mrs. Harris was about to tell. "Older than me?"

Mrs. Harris moved into the bathroom and found places on the towel rods for Sharon's wet clothes to hang.

"I was in the fifth grade. You're in fourth, right?"

"Right."

"I thought I could make it home from school. We walked to school, but it wasn't terribly far. So, I didn't take the time to use the Girls' Room at school. I didn't like school bathrooms. Anyway, I almost made it. Well, I did make it home. I even made it into the bathroom. I just didn't make it to the toilet." Mrs. Harris shook her head reminiscently. "It was very embarrassing," she added.

"But it was the last time?" Sharon asked.

"As it turned out, yes. So, I'm just supposing you already feel bad enough, and I'm not wanting to add to it."

"Yeah, you're right," Sharon admitted. She ran off toward her room for her other pair of shoes. While she was gone, Mrs. Harris took the wet shoes to the living room, where she had noticed some old newspapers on the sofa. She wadded up several sheets of newsprint, stuffed them into Sharon's shoes, then laid the shoes on the kitchen floor to dry.

When Sharon came out of her room with dry shoes on, a new question had occurred to her. "Do we have to tell Mama?"

"I think so—yes," replied Mrs. Harris. "She'll have to cope with the clothes, so she'll know. I'm certainly not going to help you lie to her. I don't think she'll be angry, do you?"

"Well," Sharon began, "why wouldn't she be?"

"She won't think you did it on purpose. I bet she'll just be sorry. Maybe she'll remember a story from her own childhood to tell you."

"Maybe," Sharon shook her head a trifle dubiously.

"You're all ready. Let's go think about lunch. We're late as it is, and I'm hungry."

They locked the door of Sharon's house, put the key back in its hiding place and walked next door where Snickers gave them his usual loud welcome. This time it didn't seem to bother Sharon at all.

Chapter 6

Conversation

Sharon finally found a way to talk about her father one afternoon the next week. They were sitting on the sofa getting ready to read. "Do you think my daddy's going to die?" she asked.

"Why? Has your mom said something?" asked Mrs. Harris.

"No, she won't talk about it."

"Have you tried?"

"Yeah, she just gets all weird. She smiles and tells me Daddy will be fine, but she just ... I don't know, she just gets weird." Sharon couldn't put into words the lack of genuineness she had felt from her mom. "Plus, she always changes the subject. What do you think? Do you think he'll die?"

Mrs. Harris considered for a moment, then closed the book most of the way, keeping her place with a finger. She looked at Sharon and said, "I'm not sure I've got any business talking to you about this. It's really your parents' job and they might be angry at me stepping in. It would be a lot better if you could ask your mom. Then again, I really don't know enough to have much of an opinion. You don't even know what he has, do you?"

"No," agreed Sharon.

"Did you tell me he's lost all his hair?"

Sharon nodded.

"Well, I wish your mom would tell you more. I've always tried to tell children the truth, so I'll tell you what I can and be honest with you, okay?"

Sharon looked up at her hopefully, and half-smiled.

"My guess is that if your dad's lost his hair, he's got some kind of cancer. Have you heard of cancer?"

Sharon's lower lip began to tremble, and Mrs. Harris put an arm around her shoulder as they sat on the sofa and pulled her closer.

"Now there are all different kinds of cancer, and some are a lot worse than others. So, we don't know if your dad's got one of the really bad ones or not," Mrs. Harris resumed. "They treat cancer with things that often make people seem really sick for a while, because they're trying to kill all the cancer cells, and anything that will kill cancer cells also makes the person pretty sick. And people usually lose their hair, which is why I think he might have cancer. Though we really don't know even that, do we?"

Sharon was looking down at the floor but shook her head, slowly, no.

"So, you see, when you treat cancer you can't help it that the person seems very sick, but it may be that the treatment will work. If it does, then he could get well."

Sharon looked up again. "Really? You really think that?"

Mrs. Harris nodded. "He could seem awfully sick now but pull through and be well again. Or maybe not. It depends on two things: one, what kind of cancer he's got, how fast-growing it is; and two, how far it had spread before they found it. Do you understand that?"

Sharon nodded yes, but she looked solemn. "Cancer—that's really bad," she said. "Are you sure?"

"I'm sure about what I told you. And the only reason I know of for him losing all his hair would be cancer treatments. But we really don't know anything, do we? And I'm not a doctor. Doctors know so much more, and it would be a lot more accurate if you heard what the doctors think. Hon, why don't you ask your mom again? Maybe just ask her what your daddy's got—if he's got cancer or what. Maybe she'd tell you if you asked."

Sharon nodded thoughtfully. "I'll try," she said, as though making a vow to herself.

Several weeks after the first library trip, Mrs. Harris invited Sharon to come to the library with her again, on the Saturday morning after Thanksgiving as it happened, to return the books Sharon had checked out on Mrs. Harris's card and maybe to check out some new ones.

Life at Sharon's house, as has been said, was very different from the tranquil, ordered existence that Mrs. Harris led. Sharon had found out, bit by bit, that Mrs. Harris did practically the same things every day.

Sharon's life was a lot more hectic. She had the routine of school, of course, which she loved, and of visiting Mrs. Harris after school, which she was coming to love, but her home life was chaotic. Breakfast was whatever she could scrounge, usually toast unless the bread had run out. Lunch was at school, and her mom tried to make something for dinner, but time was a problem, and her mother wasn't much of a cook. Boxed macaroni and cheese was sometimes the whole dinner. Or hotdogs. Or a can of baked beans heated up.

And the television was always on if Sharon's mom was awake. It was a noise in the background which had never bothered Sharon before; indeed, she had considered it completely normal until she experienced the quiet of Mrs. Harris's television-less household. The relative silence was soothing, Sharon thought.

Then, too, Sharon's mother seemed restless. There was an atmosphere of stress and unhappiness which hung over the house all the time. Sharon could remember better times if she thought back to before her dad got sick. But these days things weren't always clean, and the laundry didn't always get done. The house would get really dirty and untidy, then Mrs. Stover would clean it up and it would look nice for a few days, then it would begin to look untidy again, with things out of place. Sharon did her fair share of leaving things lying around, but she didn't like the result.

She had never realized until she started going to Mrs. Harris's house that messiness made her feel disorganized and chaotic herself. She didn't put it to herself that way. She just knew that she felt happier at Mrs. Harris's house where things seemed always to be picked up.

Sharon's own room was a marvel of disorder. Her mother's one rule was that no food should go into a bedroom. That way at least there wouldn't be bugs or mice, she said. Sharon was careful to obey this rule because she didn't like the thought of bugs or mice. And anyway, it wasn't much trouble to obey. She was always allowed to eat — just not in her room.

But even without food, her room always seemed to be a mess. Her mother rarely got around to cleaning it—never since they had moved. And Sharon, herself, was totally unable to clean it once it got beyond a certain point. The floor was four or six inches deep in dirty clothes, toys, stuffed animals, books, and trash.

So, this Saturday morning Sharon had to spend a long time searching for the library books that needed to be returned. She hadn't thought, somehow, of putting them in the tote bag that Mrs. Harris had given her for borrowed books, so she had to look everywhere. Her mother, planning to have coffee with a friend, was waiting impatiently, tapping her toe when Sharon finally found the books and was ready to head for Mrs. Harris's house. Sharon, of course, explained to Mrs. Harris that she was late because she had been looking for the library books and couldn't come until she found them.

"Where were they?" asked Mrs. Harris, as she started the car and backed out of the driveway.

"In my room," replied Sharon.

"Where in your room? Where do you keep library books?"

"Well … they sorta got under some stuff that was on the floor, and I looked everywhere else first," said Sharon. "My room's really messed up."

Mrs. Harris took her eyes off the road momentarily to glance at Sharon with a twinkle in her eye. "Do you like it that way?" she ventured.

"Like it? No, I hate it," Sharon admitted. "But it just always gets that way, and I don't know what to do. I do try sometimes," she continued, "but, I don't know, it just seems like it's too much for me."

"*Qui ne range pas, mais déplace,*" murmured Mrs. Harris.

Sharon looked at her, startled at hearing a foreign language.

"Sorry," said Mrs. Harris, stopping for a red light. "That's something a friend of mine's father once said about him. A French friend. It means, 'who doesn't put things away, just moves them around,' or more literally, 'who doesn't tidy things up but displaces them,' but it goes better in French."

"That's French?" asked Sharon.

Mrs. Harris nodded, stepping on the gas now that the light had turned green.

"I didn't know you spoke French. Say it again."

Mrs. Harris said it again.

"How come you can speak French?" Sharon wanted to know.

"Well, I studied it in school starting when I was about your age, then later my family lived in a French-speaking country for a year, so I had to speak it in school. Then I studied it some more in college. It's my favorite language, really. What about you? Are you going to study a foreign language?"

"I don't know," said Sharon. "I think maybe we study Spanish starting in junior high."

"You don't get to choose?" asked Mrs. Harris. "That's too bad. And not until junior high is almost too late. Don't get me started! But about your room, listen, I've got a couple of books that might help. Maybe we can look at them when we get back from the library."

"Yeah, okay," Sharon agreed.

"I know it's hard to clean a room that's really messy," Mrs. Harris sympathized, "but I think you're probably old enough to learn how if you want to." She laughed briefly. "At that, you'll have a head start on me. I was in my twenties before I learned how to clean up, and I learned it from one of the books I'm going to show you. It's a really good book."

Sharon was surprised to learn that Mrs. Harris hadn't always been tidy, and said so. Mrs. Harris explained that it was a lot easier now that she was by herself. Earlier in her life, with a husband and four children to look after, she hadn't always done so well.

They had almost reached the library now, so Mrs. Harris stopped talking to concentrate on parking in the underground parking garage, then they rode the elevator up to the children's floor.

Later in the morning, when they got back from the library, Mrs. Harris phoned Sharon's mother and asked if Sharon could stay longer in order to work at something. Mrs. Stover said that would be fine as long as Sharon was home by 3:30 or so to go visit her dad. In fact, she thought she might take the opportunity to do some grocery shopping. Mrs. Harris told her to go right ahead, that she would feed Sharon lunch and send her home well before 3:30.

So, Sharon and Mrs. Harris ate lunch and then read *What To Do When Your Mom or Dad Says "Clean Up Your Room"* by Joy Wilt Berry. Sharon enjoyed the book. She especially enjoyed looking for the frog on every page. The technique the book taught was quite simple but very powerful. The first step was to take everything off the bed, then to make the bed.

At this point they had to go practice bed-making on Mrs. Harris's guest room bed because the diagram of how to make a hospital corner was too much for Sharon. After unmaking and remaking the guest room bed three times, Sharon had learned a lot.

The book's next step was to start on one side of the bedroom door—in order to prevent you from standing in the middle of the room wringing your hands and saying, "Where do I start?" as Mrs Harris put it—then to go once around the room picking up everything that was out of place and putting it on the bed.

There followed a section on dusting and vacuuming. Mrs. Harris showed Sharon how to dust and promised to send her home with some dust cloths and a can of aerosol dusting spray. Sharon practiced vacuuming too, learning how to go over each part of the carpet twice.

Snickers hated the vacuum cleaner. "A lot of dogs do," said Mrs. Harris. "I think it hurts his ears." After he had staged three stealth-and-grab attacks on it, Mrs. Harris took pity on him and put him outside.

The last step was to take things off the bed one by one, and put each thing where it belonged, whether away in a drawer, or in the laundry or trash, or in a box of things to be given away.

"And once you pick a thing up," Mrs. Harris reminded Sharon, "it's important not to put it down again until it's where it belongs. That's the key to the whole process, really. If you follow that rule, the method that this book teaches will really work. You'll have a clean room."

"I can't wait to try," said Sharon. "As soon as I get home."

"Well, now, don't go too fast," warned Mrs. Harris. "If your room is as messy as you say it is, you might want to wait till tomorrow because once you start you can't go to bed until you finish, you know. There'll be stuff all over your bed. Anyway, you're going to visit your dad today, right?"

Sharon thought about that. "Maybe in the morning would be better," she agreed.

"Don't forget either," added Mrs. Harris, "that there's a second part of the book which we haven't read yet. So, you clean up your room first, but if it gives you a lot of trouble don't be upset. There are further measures that can be taken after it's clean. The extra part of the book is called something like, 'If you had a lot of trouble cleaning up your room.'"

Sharon nodded. "I'll remember."

"And there's a Berenstain Bears book that might be helpful, too," concluded Mrs. Harris. "We can read it on Monday."

Chapter 7

Sharon Cleans Her Room

The next day, Sunday, Sharon was up bright and early, ready to start on her room. The clattering she made moving things, especially the rather premature dragging of the vacuum cleaner down the hall, woke her mother up and brought her to the doorway of Sharon's room to see what was happening.

"What in the world?" Mrs. Stover asked sleepily, seeing the bed-clothes stripped off the bed. She was wearing a hastily donned bath-robe, and her hair was all on end.

"Mrs. Harris taught me how to clean my room, and I'm going to do it," said Sharon happily.

"Uh," Mrs. Stover grunted, in a disbelieving way. "Try to be a little quieter about it, okay? I'm trying to sleep in. I'll be interested to see if it works," she added, casting a doubtful look at the messy room.

Sharon went back to work. Having already stripped the bed, she found some clean sheets and made it up fresh. This was hard to do as the bed was in a corner of the room. Then she followed the book's instructions. Beginning, in her case, to the immediate left of the bed-room door she picked up everything that was out of place—every-thing really—and put the things on her bed. There were dirty clothes, clean clothes, toys, books, school papers, all sorts of things.

She was left with a pretty dirty room. It hadn't been cleaned since they moved in, which was almost eight weeks ago now. Using the borrowed dusting spray and three rags, she dusted her toy box, the chest of drawers, the table that she used for a desk, and the head-board of her bed. Then she vacuumed the whole room. By now her mother had given up on trying to sleep and was making coffee.

After vacuuming, Sharon figured she deserved a break, so she put the vacuum cleaner back in the hall closet and went to see what she could find for breakfast. And after breakfast, she looked at the Sunday comics.

But the unfinished room drew her back. She was soon at work again, taking a green plastic garbage bag with her and a laundry bas-ket. First, she picked all the dirty clothes off the bed, that being most of them, put them in the laundry basket and took them down the hall to the hamper outside the bathroom door. She couldn't stuff them all in, but at least piled them there.

Then she went back to her room and picked trash off the bed, putting it in the garbage bag—lots of old school papers, used-up col-oring books, broken crayons, broken toys, and toys that had come free with fast-food meals and which she didn't want any more.

That left the clean clothes, the good toys, and some books. Sha-ron dusted the toys off one by one and put them in the toy box. She got a shock when she opened the toy box lid, to see how full it already was, but not as big as the shock she got when she opened her closet door to hang some clothes in it. There was a big jumble of things on the floor—not just clothes either—all sorts of things. On the other hand, hardly anything was hung up, so she had no trouble finding the few hangers she needed.

She didn't have a bookcase, so she dusted her books and stood them across the back of her table, up against the wall. Having now cleared everything off the bed, Sharon smoothed out the bedclothes, which had gotten wrinkled in the process of putting things on the bed and taking them off again. Then she went to call her mom.

Mrs. Stover came down the hallway with her daughter and stopped dead on the threshold of the room. "My goodness, Sharon!" she exclaimed. "How in the world did you make it look so good?" She hugged Sharon close.

"I told you, Mama, Mrs. Harris taught me out of a book," came the somewhat muffled voice of her daughter, whose face was pressed against her mother's midriff.

"A book? What book?" asked Mrs. Stover.

"It's called something like *What To Do When Your Mom or Dad Says 'Pick Up Your Room'*" replied Sharon.

"What a wonderful idea for a book! I never dreamed you could do such a good job. Maybe I'll start telling you to do it sometimes, now that you've read the book," joked Sharon's mother.

"I was thinking, Mama, I bet we could do the same thing with the living room if we used the sofa," suggested Sharon. "Only not today 'cause I'm tired."

Her mom didn't understand all of this but replied to the part she did understand. "You deserve some rest. Let's figure out lunch, then we'll go see your daddy."

Over lunch, Sharon took courage from all the praise her mother had showered on her about her room and asked what was wrong with her dad. Even so, it was a hard thing for her to do. She felt kind of dizzy from her heart beating so fast, and she didn't know how white her face was and how young she really looked, as she sat at the table, spoon in hand. "Please, Mama, I'm old enough to know and I think it makes me even scareder not knowing, 'cause I know it's something bad."

Mrs. Stover stopped eating and looked up from her tomato soup, troubled. She thought for a long moment, but then explained, rather hesitantly, that Sharon's dad had leukemia, cancer of the bone marrow.

"Is he going to be all right?" Sharon wanted to know. "Mrs. Harris and I talked, and she told me he probably had cancer because I said all his hair had fallen out, and she said people with cancer can look really, really sick because of the treatments, but sometimes they get better, even maybe completely well, in the end."

"We just don't know, Sharon," sighed her mother. "The doctors haven't given up hope yet, if they can just get him back into remission. That means getting the cancer to go away. But we just don't know. He had something called a bone marrow transplant before we moved to this house. Remember when I got that babysitter to come stay with you for a couple of days?"

"Yeah," Sharon nodded.

"But then he came out of remission after that."

"So that's bad, right?" asked Sharon.

Her mother nodded.

"Is he going to come home again soon?" Sharon wanted to know.

"Not too soon, I don't think," replied her mother. "I'll tell you when I find out."

Sharon felt both better and worse. She had known it was something bad, but it was still, somehow, a shock to have it put into words.

When they went to visit her father that afternoon, the first thing Sharon's mom said, right after she kissed Sharon's dad was, "She knows, Jim. She asked, and I told her."

Sharon's father held out his arms to Sharon, and she forced herself to go over and give him a hug. She was shocked by how bony he felt, even though she knew just by looking at him that he was thin. But when she listened to him, he still sounded like her dad.

"I'm sorry, Baby, he said now, patting Sharon's back. "I didn't want you to be bothered with it." Sharon could hear the tears in his voice.

"But Daddy, I knew you were real sick," she protested. "It's made me scared all the time, but I don't think it's any worse knowing what it is. Maybe it's better even."

"But you're only eight years old, Baby."

"I've turned nine, Daddy," interjected Sharon.

"Well, okay, nine then," said her dad. "But that's not very old. I wish you didn't have to know about it. Hell, I wish it wasn't happening even," he added, mostly to himself. "But I promise you this, Hon. I'm going to beat this if it's a possible thing. I'm fighting as hard as I can. Don't stop coming to see me now, okay? I love seeing you every weekend and hearing what you've been doing, you hear me?"

"Okay, Daddy," sobbed Sharon. After a minute, Sharon's father leaned back on the bed and reached for a Kleenex to blow his nose. Sharon took one, too.

Her mother helped them pull themselves together by remarking, "You'd never guess what Sharon did this morning, Jim."

"What's that?" he asked, letting the Kleenex drop into the wastepaper basket by his bed.

"She cleaned up her room, all by herself—did a really good job, too."

"Well now, that's nice to hear," said Sharon's dad. "You're getting to be a big girl if you can do something like that all by yourself."

"Oh, Daddy," protested Sharon. "Of course, I'm a big girl."

"Not all that big, Hon," said her dad. "Not to me."

That was the best visit they'd had in a long time. Somehow, Sharon wasn't so shocked by his appearance once they talked honestly about his illness, and he, too, seemed to have more to say to her now that the secret of his illness wasn't standing between them. Sharon stayed in the hospital room longer than she usually did, though in the end she did go out in the hallway and read while her parents spent more time together.

The next day being Monday, Sharon had a lot to tell Mrs. Harris on the way home from school. First, she talked about her dad having leukemia and all about what her mother had said. Then, she told her about visiting her dad, and that he had been interested to hear about the room-cleaning book and all the other reading that she and Mrs. Harris did.

"I told him how much fun it is," she said, "and how many cool books you know."

Mrs. Harris smiled. "Well, I've been at it a long time," she pointed out. "I really never quit reading children's books, just added grown-up ones, and then my own children came along. A good book, one that has that spark that makes it a really good book, well, people of any age can enjoy it. That's what I think anyway."

Of course, Sharon told about her clean room, and how impressed her mom had been.

"Was it hard to do?" asked Mrs. Harris.

"Well…" Sharon thought for a few seconds. Then, "It worked," she said slowly, "only the thing is that my closet is still a big mess. So are my drawers and toy box. And I don't have a bookcase, so I had to put the books on my table. They look pretty good, though."

Mrs. Harris offered to free up a small bookcase which was holding old *Reader's Digests* in her garage. They went straight to the garage when they arrived at Mrs. Harris's house. Mrs. Harris emptied the bookcase, spreading its *Reader's Digests* out between the two other little garage bookcases. She dusted the now-empty bookcase. Then she and Sharon carried it next door, used the hidden key, and took it down the hallway to Sharon's bedroom where it fitted nicely next to her bed. Mrs. Harris admired how clean the room looked but saw the problem with the overstuffed toy box and closet.

"Let's read the second part of the book," she suggested.

"Yeah, let's see what it says."

They went back to Mrs. Harris's house for a snack and reading.

SHARON'S ROOM

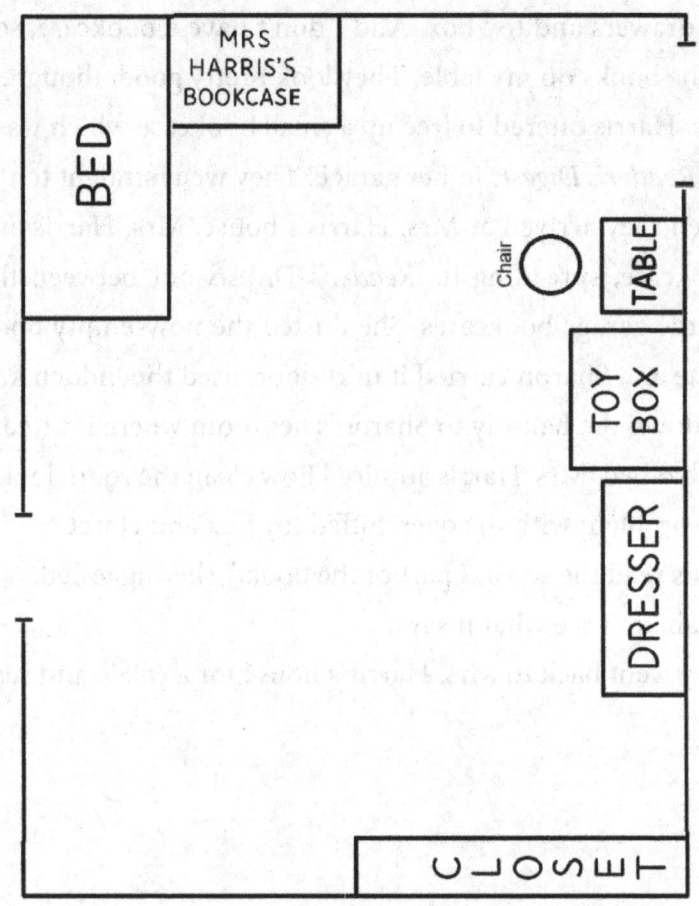

Chapter 8

Advent

The first thing Sharon noticed when they walked into Mrs. Harris's kitchen was an evergreen wreath with a shiny red bow, which was sitting on the kitchen table. There were four candles spaced around the wreath, three of them purple and one pink.

"How pretty!" exclaimed Sharon. "What is it?"

"It's called an Advent wreath," answered Mrs. Harris. "Advent started yesterday."

"What's Advent?"

"It's the start of the Church year. You know how the year starts on January first, New Year's Day, right?"

"Right."

"Well, the Church has a year, too, but it's different from the regular year. Instead of months it's got seasons—six of them. The Church year starts with Advent, and Advent usually comes right at the end of November, just after Thanksgiving.

It was true that Thanksgiving had been the previous Thursday. Sharon hadn't enjoyed it at all this year. Not only had it been boring, but in her opinion, it hadn't been a Thanksgiving at all. Mrs. Harris had gone to visit friends in a nearby city. She was gone just for Thursday and Friday.

Luckily, Sharon's mother was off work both days. Sharon hadn't had to stay alone, but all her mother seemed to do these days was watch TV if she wasn't working or visiting Sharon's dad.

On Thanksgiving Day itself, they had gone to a restaurant, then had spent the whole afternoon at the hospital. Sharon had hated going to a restaurant for Thanksgiving dinner. The food wasn't even all that good, and it didn't feel like Thanksgiving to her to be eating in a restaurant instead of having a family dinner. So, it had been a really bad Thanksgiving, Sharon thought, the worst she could remember.

Mrs. Harris went on explaining. "We light one candle, one of the purple ones, for the first week of Advent, which is this one. Next week we'll light two, then three, and so on. When we're lighting all four it will be just a few days until Christmas."

"It's neat," said Sharon.

"Would you like to be the one to light the candle?" asked Mrs. Harris.

"Me?" Sharon was horrified. "That's dangerous! They're always telling us not to play with matches."

Mrs. Harris nodded. "I'm right here watching. You wouldn't be playing with matches; you'd be using them. And it's not dangerous if you're careful."

Sharon shook her head.

"Let me do it today, but you watch me," said Mrs. Harris. "You're about the right age for learning how to do this. I learned when I was eight or nine. And I was scared at first, too."

She took a box of kitchen matches out of a drawer and lit the purple candle opposite to the pink one, talking every step of the way about what she was doing.

"I open the box and pull out a match." She demonstrated. "Then I close the box to make sure the other matches don't catch on fire when I light this one." She slid the cover back over the box. "This strip along the side is what you light the match on. It usually takes several tries." She struck the match on the strip. It burst into flame on the second try.

"Isn't that neat how that happens?" she asked. "Notice how I grabbed the end of the match as far away as I could from the head before I lit it," she commented, as she held the match to the wick of a purple candle. "You wait until you can see that the candle's going to light, then you blow the match out," she added, suiting her actions to the words.

"But keep an eye on the match," she cautioned. "They're not very long, and sometimes you just have to blow it out and light another one before the candle lights. Now, I put the burned out match in the sink rather than the trash. I want to be sure it's really out before I throw it away. It can't do any harm in the sink one way or the other."

Sharon had paid close attention.

"What do you think?" Mrs. Harris asked. "Does that look like something you could do?"

"I don't know," said Sharon. "Maybe. Sometime. Not tomorrow," she added quickly. "I want to watch you again."

After snack, Mrs. Harris let Sharon blow out the candle, then they moved into the living room where Sharon noticed another new thing. On the mantel there was a whole little scene with a building, figures of a man and a woman, some shepherds, a donkey, an ox, even some sheep. It looked as though it would be fun to play with.

"What's that?" Sharon wanted to know.

"Haven't you ever seen a nativity set?" Mrs. Harris asked, surprised.

"I guess not. Well, maybe somewhere," Sharon remembered. "They're for Christmas, aren't they?"

"Christmas, yes, but it starts in Advent, like the wreaths," answered Mrs. Harris.

Sharon stood on tiptoe to examine the nativity set more closely. "Where's the baby? And aren't there supposed to be camels?"

"The baby won't be born until Christmas," said Mrs. Harris. "Oh, I know some people put him in the crèche anyway, but Catholics often don't. I always have the nativity set out from Advent until after Epiphany, so He'll have plenty of time to be there."

"What's Epi-epi-… what you said?" asked Sharon.

"It's part of the Church year again. Like I was talking about with Advent. Advent is first, then comes Christmas, then Epiphany when the Wise Men arrive on camels to visit the baby Jesus."

"Could I maybe play with it?" asked Sharon.

"As long as you're careful," Mrs. Harris replied, then smiled. "As a matter of fact, I put it on a tray this year because it did just occur to me that you might want to play with it. Let me put Snickers out—I don't trust him with anything like this. He might decide to chew on one of the pieces."

She returned shortly, picked up the tray with the nativity set on it, and set it down carefully in front of the fireplace.

"So, where are the camels?" remembered Sharon. "Aren't there any camels?"

"Of course, there are camels—and Magi—Kings," she added, seeing the question in Sharon's eyes. "The Wise Men. They don't arrive until Epiphany as I said. They're in my study. They'll be traveling all over the house until January 6th. You can help me to move them a little every day, just so we keep them up high enough to be out of Snickers's reach. Come see."

Sharon followed Mrs. Harris down the hallway to her study, which she had hardly ever seen. It was a smallish room with a computer, an easy chair, a desk and, of course, a whole lot of books. On one of the bookshelves, in front of the books, were camels and Wise Men. There were three of each, all different. One camel was being ridden by a white-bearded king. Another camel was standing without a rider, and the third was kneeling. All three kings were different, too. Besides the white-bearded king there was a black man. The third king was a younger-looking man. The camels' trappings were of beautiful colors and the whole group seemed to be camped at an oasis. There were a couple of palm trees, only eight or nine inches high, and a pavilion, or open tent, which was made of rich fabrics, gorgeously-colored silks and brocades.

Sharon was enthralled. "Can I really help move them every day?"

"Yes, of course, dear. I told you you could."

"Have they already moved today, or can I do it?"

"They might like to go a little farther," allowed Mrs. Harris, smiling with her eyes. "If you want them to."

So, Sharon very carefully moved Wise Men, camels, palm trees, and the pavilion to the next bookcase nearer the door and up one shelf.

Then they went back to the living room. Sharon played with the main part of the nativity set for a few minutes while Mrs. Harris started reading the second part of the book about how to clean your room. Soon, though, the need to look at the pictures in the book, especially finding the boy's frog on each page and seeing what funny thing it was doing this time, drew her to the sofa next to Mrs. Harris. Besides, a sound of scratching at the kitchen door had started, so Mrs. Harris put the nativity set back up on the mantel and went to let Snickers in from the back yard.

The second part of the book explained how to organize your things, sorting out what you really wanted and were using from the outgrown or otherwise useless clothes and toys. After that book, they read *The Berenstain Bears and the Messy Room*, which advocated finding storage containers for each kind of toy: a shoebox for toy dinosaurs, one for each puzzle, a box for blocks, one for art supplies, etc. It sounded good.

"I think I'll wait a few days to try it, though," Sharon said.

Chapter 9

God and Sunday School

"Are you scared of dying?" Sharon asked Mrs. Harris, a day or two later, as they were sitting at the kitchen table having snack.

Mrs. Harris gave her a considering look. She knew that Sharon was really asking about her father. She thought for a few seconds before replying. "I'm not scared of being dead," she said finally, "because I know God and I trust Him, but I think everyone's afraid of dying, at least a little afraid, because it might hurt and because it's so strange that we can't imagine it: such a big step, even bigger in a way than being born."

Sharon mulled that over. "I don't remember being born."

"No, people don't," agreed Mrs. Harris. "At least, they don't remember it past their early childhoods."

"What do you think happens when you die?" persisted the girl.

"You see God. That's what happens," declared Mrs. Harris.

"I don't think I believe in God," said Sharon.

"Yes, you said that once before," commented Mrs. Harris. "Luckily, He believes in you." She chuckled.

"What do you mean?"

"Sorry, that's a bad joke. I'm not making fun of you. You don't know God yet, but that's not to say you never will. I didn't know Him when I was your age, and I used to wonder a lot if there was a God. God made you—He made everything—so, of course, He believes in you. That's what I meant."

"How do you know that?" wondered Sharon.

"That's who God is. Did anyone ever teach you anything about Him?"

"I guess not. Daddy says 'Oh, God!' sometimes when he's angry, but that's all."

"You don't go to church, then?" questioned Mrs. Harris.

"No, we never did, but this one time I stayed overnight with a friend, and they took me to church the next morning, but I didn't like it much. It scared me, really, because I had to go down in a basement, and it smelled funny and it was kind of dark down there. And then we went into this little room, and a lady was there, and she had this weird thing like a cloth board with pictures she put on it, and they stuck…"

"A flannel board," suggested Mrs. Harris.

"Yeah, I guess. Well, I'd never seen one, and there weren't any windows in the room, or they were painted over or something. But I guess what really scared me was that everybody else, all the other kids I mean, they seemed to know what she was talking about, and they could answer her questions and stuff, and I didn't know anything. I just sat by my friend the whole time. Then, after a long time, they gave us juice and crackers, and then we got to go. So, that's the only time I ever went to church, and I didn't really learn anything."

"I see," said Mrs. Harris. "You went to Sunday school, not church. Church is completely different. It was the same for me. It took me a long time to learn about God because my parents didn't know anything about Him. I didn't go to church either when I was little."

"So, who is God?" Sharon asked again.

"God is the one who made everything," repeated Mrs. Harris. "We're alive because He made us. He made the stars, the planets, the people, the animals, the plants, the mountains, the oceans—everything."

"Wow," said Sharon. "Do people know anything about Him? How did you find out?"

"It took me a long time," admitted Mrs. Harris, "but I always wanted to know about Him, if He was really true and, in the end, I found Him. Or He found me," she added. "He promises that He will. 'You will seek me and find me, when you seek me with all your heart. I will be found by you,' says the Lord," she quoted. "That's in the Bible.

"Although in my experience," she went on, "you'll find Him if you're even willing to know the truth. It may take a while, though. We can talk more about this another day. There's a lot to know about God, more than you can take in during one talk. Why don't you just think about what I've said, and we can come back to it. Let's get to reading."

They were in the middle of *A Morgan for Melinda* by Doris Gates and were both looking forward to the day's installment. It was another book about a fearful girl who overcame her fears, in this case her fear of horses. They moved into the living room and didn't talk any more about God that day.

They came back to the topic of God, though, at least for a few minutes, almost every day. Also, Mrs. Harris managed to catch Sharon's mother alone again and got her permission to talk with Sharon about God. She found out that Sharon's father was a lapsed Catholic and her mother a not-very-committed Episcopalian.

"I don't really think it matters what you believe, as long as you believe something," asserted Mrs. Stover, a statement with which Mrs. Harris disagreed so profoundly that she was rendered speechless.

But Sharon's mom said she didn't mind if Mrs. Harris talked to Sharon about God. And Mrs. Harris broached the idea of having Sharon meet a priest from her parish church, to see if he could say anything helpful to Sharon about her fears.

Mrs. Stover said she would mention it to her husband, but she didn't see what harm it could do, so Mrs. Harris made plans to invite a priest friend, Fr. Karimu, to tea as soon as he could find time to come—that very week if possible. She would need to present it to Sharon carefully, though, in order not to scare her.

In their talks about God, Sharon learned that Jesus is God's Son and that He founded the Church. She learned about the Bible. Mrs. Harris told her stories about how she had come to believe and promised to pray for Sharon. "My grandmother and aunt were always praying for me and for my brothers and cousins," she said, "and I suspect that it helped a lot. Maybe it's why I was always interested in God."

Mrs. Harris moved so quickly in inviting her priest friend because she continued to be worried about Sharon. So many things frightened her! It seemed to Mrs. Harris that fear ruled her life. Sharon was almost never really relaxed. She seemed to be perpetually alert to the smallest sound, constantly analyzing the world around her for the dangers she expected to encounter. This was less notice-able at Mrs. Harris's house, now that Sharon had gotten used to it, but it became really pronounced when they were out in public or if their routine changed in any way. Worse yet, Mrs. Harris noticed that Sharon quite often shook, just a little. Sharon herself did her best to ignore the shaking and get on with life, but Mrs. Harris was deeply concerned for her, and hoped that, between Fr. Karimu and prayer, Sharon could be helped.

When she asked Sharon if she had ever met a priest, Sharon an-swered that she didn't think so, then asked what a priest was.

"Well, it's a little hard to explain. I've got a good friend who's a priest, and I've invited him to tea so you can meet him," said Mrs. Harris. "Your mom said that would be okay. Luckily, he's free to-morrow. He's a very kind man, and I think you'll probably like him. He's good at talking about God too. You can ask him things."

"What is a priest?" Sharon repeated the question. "I mean, I've heard the word, but I don't really know what it means."

"A priest is a man who has given his whole life to God, to serve Him," answered Mrs. Harris. "That's part of the answer to your question. Priests never marry or have children of their own, at least Catholic priests never do, and that means they can be a father, a spir-itual father, to all of us. That's why we always call them 'Father'."

"Really?" Sharon was intrigued.

Mrs. Harris nodded. "You'll meet him tomorrow."

Sharon had largely accepted Mrs. Harris as a fact of nature, as most children do with most grown-ups, not asking any questions about her background, even in her own mind. Oh, she had found out a little about how she spent her time, but had not learned much about Mrs. Harris's past, beyond the fact that she had four children. There were pictures of the children at various ages lining the walls of her hallway. And Sharon had been surprised to learn that Mrs. Harris spoke French. But that was really all she knew. Otherwise, it was as though she thought Mrs. Harris had always lived in the place Sharon had found her when they moved into the little house next door.

Meeting Fr. Karimu made Sharon more curious about Mrs. Harris's past life. She realized that she actually knew next to nothing about her.

Chapter 10

Tanzania

The questions started the next day when they were walking home from school together, Snickers capering about on the end of the leash as always. Mrs. Harris sometimes compared his leash manners to having a trout on the end of a fishing line, as he pulled first this way, then that. This particular day, Mrs. Harris reminded Sharon that they could expect Fr. Karimu to tea and said that they had better read first if they wanted to read at all—which of course they did.

So, Sharon dashed to move the Wise Men and camels as soon as they got to Mrs. Harris's house. Then they sat in front of the fireplace, with a nice log fire burning, and read for about forty minutes. Sharon stared at the fire (she loved watching the flames) and listened to the reading until Fr. Karimu arrived.

"He'll be late," predicted Mrs. Harris. "I invited him for 4:30, but Africans are mostly late."

"Is he African?" Sharon asked, startled.

"Yes, didn't I tell you? He's from a country called Tanzania in East Africa, where Mt. Kilimanjaro is," replied Mrs. Harris. "I'll have to show you a picture of it sometime."

When Fr. Karimu came to the door, Sharon saw a large, cheerful black man with a friendly smile, who was wearing ordinary clothes except for what is called a "Roman collar," but on him the collar was unfastened and hung open around his neck, giving him more room to breathe.

To Sharon's great surprise, syllables of a different language started coming out of Mrs. Harris's mouth: *"Tumsifu Yesu Kristu, Padre. Karibu!"*

"Milele amina, Dada. Asante," returned the priest.

"Habari za siku nyingi?"

"Salama tu. Na wewe, je?"

"Na mimi pia. Salama tu."

They stood in the entryway of Mrs. Harris's house, facing each other and holding hands while they chatted. Sharon's eyes went back and forth to whichever one was speaking at the moment, her mouth slightly agape, her eyes large with surprise. She heard her own name twice, but, of course, understood nothing else.

Finally, Fr. Karimu dropped Mrs. Harris's hand and offered a hand the size of a baseball mitt to Sharon. She shook hands hesitantly, but he didn't let go, just smiled at her and asked her, in English but with quite a strong accent, how she was.

Sharon replied that she was fine, thank you, but looked up at Mrs. Harris for reassurance.

"What were you speaking?" The pent-up question came out in a rush.

"That is Swahili," answered Mrs. Harris. "It's the language they mainly speak in Tanzania."

"You speak Swahili, too? And French? And English?"

Mrs. Harris nodded. "I speak quite a lot of Swahili. Not perfectly though," she added, at which a protest burst from Fr. Karimu, but again in what Sharon now knew to be Swahili.

Mrs. Harris smiled at him and said something back.

The priest smiled at Sharon and spoke to her. "She speaks very good Swahili," he pronounced.

"Now let's go to the kitchen and have some tea," suggested Mrs. Harris. "Sharon and I have been waiting for you, and we're pretty hungry."

They walked down the hall to the kitchen, where Sharon saw that the kitchen table was already laid for a special tea, with a cake reposing on a plate in the center of the table. This explained why Mrs. Harris had left Snickers outside while they read.

Fr. Karimu washed his hands in the small bathroom next to the kitchen, so Sharon washed hers, too. Then they sat down.

Fr. Karimu said the same prayer that Mrs. Harris always said before starting to eat ("Bless us, O Lord, and these Thy gifts, which we are about to receive from Thy bounty, through Christ, Our Lord. Amen,") and both of them crossed themselves twice, once at the beginning and once at the end of it.

Besides the cake, there was hot water in a thermos to make tea with, hot milk in a smaller thermos, and lots of other things on the table: tea bags in a glass jar, sugar, bread and butter, jam, and a basket of fruit which Sharon saw contained bananas, oranges, and a fruit she didn't recognize, but which Mrs. Harris told her was called a papaya.

"Just like Tanzania," remarked Fr. Karimu, looking around with pleasure and smiling broadly as he took a tea bag, put it into his tea cup, and poured hot water from the thermos over it.

Sharon was given her usual glass of milk, then watched in wide-eyed wonder as the priest put one, two, three, four spoonfuls of sugar into his tea. She had never seen anybody put more than two in a cup of tea before and wasn't sure it was possible to put that much in and have it dissolve.

Mrs. Harris caught Sharon's look and smiled at her with her eyes, but replied to the comment the priest had made. "You know I always try to set a table like in Tanzania for you, Father," she said. "The cake is extra, of course, because I know how much you like it."

Then she turned her attention to Sharon and gave her a piece of bread which she had already buttered.

"How come you know how things are in Tanzania?" Sharon wondered out loud.

"I lived there for several years, Sharon," replied Mrs. Harris. "Didn't you know that? … No, I guess not," she answered her own question. "Come to think of it, you haven't asked me much about myself, and I haven't told you much either, have I?"

Sharon shook her head, unable to speak because her mouth was full.

"Well, I will some time if you want me to," promised Mrs. Harris.

"Mama Wilma (only he said 'Weel-mah') was a great help to my community," Fr. Karimu said.

Mrs. Harris demurred, shaking her head. "I loved every minute of it, and I think the community helped me more than I helped it."

"Every minute?" he teased her. "Rats? Malaria?"

"I didn't often get malaria," Mrs. Harris pointed out.

But Sharon was even more surprised than before. "Aren't you scared of anything?" she asked Mrs. Harris. "If I saw a rat, I'd just die!" And she repeated, "Aren't you scared of *anything*?"

"I don't like rats," admitted Mrs. Harris. "Yes, I could be scared of a rat under the right circumstances. Or maybe the wrong ones? But, really, Sharon, that's not enough reason to stay out of Africa, just because there are some rats."

"It would be for me," declared Sharon.

"For that matter, this country has rats, too," Mrs. Harris pointed out. "There are places around here that have them, even."

"Are there?" Fr. Karimu was interested. "I have never seen a rat in this country." He helped himself to a piece of the cake and began to eat it.

"You go to the slums of any large city, and you'll see some," said Mrs. Harris. "But maybe that's enough about rats," she continued, giving Fr. Karimu a warning look because she had noticed Sharon beginning to seem anxious, looking around the room in a worried way and with her feet pulled well up off the floor.

"Anyway, the heat was the hardest part about living in Africa for me. I didn't know it was possible for a human being to sweat so much until I went to Africa."

Fr. Karimu laughed, showing a lot of very white teeth. "I remember how hard it was for you," he said.

They talked about the heat and humidity in Moshi, a city where they both had lived, agreed that Morogoro was even hotter, and told Sharon that Tanzania was so near the equator that there really weren't any seasons—just rainy times and dry times of the year.

Sharon's thoughts drifted while the adults reminisced. Finally, she waited for a pause in the conversation and asked Mrs. Harris the question that had been preoccupying her, "Do you do things even if you're scared? How can you? If I'm scared, I can't do things."

Mrs. Harris looked at her steadily. "I've seen you do things in spite of your fear. Like feeding Snickers a dog biscuit that first day when you met him."

"Oh," Sharon admitted. "Yeah, but going to Africa! And rats!"

"And you lit the candle on the Advent wreath yesterday, didn't you? You were scared but you did it."

It was true that Sharon had lit the candle the day before. She had been pretty tense, but it had worked. She had done it."

"Well, yeah, I did."

"If I think God wants me to do something, then I try not to let fear stop me. I just trust God to take care of me. Pretty much, I do that anyway. But to be fair, Sharon, I didn't know there *were* rats in Tanzania before I went there."

Fr. Karimu smiled, "But you weren't scared of the lizards, were you? Do you remember the German priests who visited? They started shouting and about six of us went running to the guest house, thinking that someone was being killed. Do you remember?"

Mrs. Harris laughed, nodding, then got up from the table to let Snickers in. He'd been scratching at the back door increasingly loudly. She paused halfway to the back door. "It was a gecko, wasn't it? They'd seen a gecko on the wall?"

"What's a gecko?" Sharon wanted to know.

Mrs. Harris had reached the door by now. When she opened it, Snickers came rushing in, as usual, like a small, white whirlwind. He tore around greeting everyone. Fr. Karimu seemed a special favorite as he leaned over and petted the little dog kindly. Mrs. Harris got a dog biscuit out for Snickers, who took it over to the carpet in the hall and settled down to eat it.

They returned to the subject of geckos.

"A gecko is a small lizard, the kind that can walk on walls and even ceilings. They're a plain little khaki-colored lizard—that's tan," she explained to Sharon, "with beady black eyes. And supposedly they have suction-cups on their toes that make them able to walk across ceilings. There was generally one in every room, and we always liked to have them around because they eat insects, and anything that eats insects is a good thing in Africa."

"Especially anything that eats mosquitos," put in Fr. Karimu.

"Yes, especially mosquitos because some of them are carrying malaria. That's a disease. A lot of people get malaria in Tanzania, and it can be pretty serious."

"So those priests were yelling because of one of them?" Sharon asked.

Fr. Karimu nodded, smiling widely again. "Two big men—imagine! Scared of a little lizard."

Sharon smiled, too, but wanted to know how big a gecko was. Fr. Karimu showed her, indicating that they were four or five inches long.

"Some are much smaller, though," Mrs. Harris remembered. "And they're scared of people. It seemed as though every time one of them caught sight of me it would just panic—be like, 'Oh, no!'" She made the face of a lizard being appalled at the sight of a person. "Then it would do something stupid: fall off the wall, or run across my foot or something."

Fr. Karimu took a banana and a piece of bread. He began to spread butter on the bread while Mrs. Harris cut up the papaya, slitting it lengthwise, a little like cutting up a watermelon.

Sharon was surprised to see that the inside of the papaya was full of round black seeds, about the size of BBs. The flesh of the papaya itself was coral colored and looked juicy. Mrs. Harris picked up a spoon and gently scraped the seeds away from one papaya crescent, then put it on Fr. Karimu's plate.

"This looks like a good one to me," she said with a smile as she cut off a second wedge. "It can be hard to get them ripe enough in this country. I've been ripening this one in a paper bag for several days. Would you care to try a bite?" she asked Sharon.

Sharon nodded, so Mrs. Harris cut a triangle off the end of her crescent after she had scraped its seeds out. She put the triangle on Sharon's plate, saying, "You don't eat its skin. Just scoop the soft part out with a spoon, like this," and she demonstrated on her part of the papaya, scooping out a mouthful of it with her spoon. "It *is* a good one," she commented when she had swallowed it.

Fr. Karimu nodded agreement, his mouth full.

Sharon nibbled at her papaya. It was sweet, but her mind didn't seem to know how to categorize it.

Mrs. Harris laughed at the expression on Sharon's face. "You don't know what to think of it, do you?" she asked. "It's an unfamiliar taste."

Sharon agreed, "It's sweet, but I can't decide what it tastes like."

"Give yourself time to get used to it," advised Mrs. Harris. "If you have it again another day, your mind will have sorted things out and then you can decide if you like it or not."

Fr. Karimu started to make himself another cup of tea. He smiled at Sharon and said, "Mama Wilma tells me that you are wanting to know more about God. Is that true?"

Sharon looked up at his friendly face and couldn't be scared of him, in spite of his bigness and brownness.

"I want to know why Mrs. Harris feels so safe," she said slowly. "I mean, why can she make me feel so safe? If that's God, then I want to know about Him. But I don't know anything, really. Is He really, truly real?"

Fr. Karimu nodded, then explained, as Mrs. Harris had, that God is the Maker of everything that is. He pointed out that everything has to have a maker. If you see a table or a chair you know that somebody made it, and it's the same with mountains and oceans, trees, animals, and people.

Then he told her the story of Adam and Eve, how they rebelled against God's command and brought death into the world. "Death is the worst enemy of all," said Fr. Karimu.

Sharon had been listening, looking down at the table. Now she looked up with a troubled face and said, "My daddy has cancer and I'm afraid he's going to die. I think about it all the time. Because I don't know what happens when you die. But I know it's something bad, and it can happen to anyone, any time."

Fr. Karimu reached across the table and took Sharon's hand. Sharon had already noticed that Tanzanians seemed to be very hand-holding people. "So, you are seeing what a terrible enemy death is, aren't you? Do you know what it took to beat death?"

Sharon shook her head, not understanding the question. Death had been beaten?

Fr. Karimu explained that God, Himself, had to come down to earth and die so that death could be conquered. God was the only One who could do it. Every person was a sinner because of Adam.

And he explained that sin means rebelling against God and wanting your own way instead of His way—things like being selfish or greedy, thinking of yourself instead of thinking of others.

He continued, explaining how God loved people so much that He was willing to do what it took so that we could go to heaven, and how He was crucified but then was resurrected on the third day, as the Bible said. He talked a little about what the Bible was, then said that was surely enough for one day.

"You think things over," he added. "I will pray for you, and you should pray, too. Tell God you want to know if He is real. He will find a way to show you that He is."

"I don't know how to pray," protested Sharon. "How can I pray to God if I don't know that He's real?"

"Just pretend that He is there and talk to Him," suggested Fr. Karimu. "You could say, 'God, if you are real, please show me the truth about You.'"

"He always answers that prayer, but you have to be patient," remarked Mrs. Harris, who had been amazingly quiet while all this went on. "It might seem as though it takes Him a while to answer. I'll pray, too, Sharon. Don't you worry about it—God will show you that He exists."

"And you ask Mama Wilma any questions that you think of," concluded Fr. Karimu. "I'll come back sometime soon, but maybe she will bring you to Mass, if your parents will let you come."

"Would you like that?" asked Mrs. Harris.

"I think so, maybe," answered Sharon. "But I don't know if Mama would let me."

"We can ask," said Mrs. Harris. "I think she might well. After all, your father was raised Catholic."

"Was he?" Fr. Karimu was interested.

He and Mrs. Harris stood talking for a few minutes about news of people in Tanzania and elsewhere. Then, he left, and soon after that Sharon's mother came home from work, and Sharon crossed back to her own house. She wasn't very hungry for dinner after the late snack with all the good food.

The next day, of course, Mrs. Harris wanted to know what Sharon had thought of meeting Fr. Karimu. They were walking home from school in a nasty sleeting rain, both of them all bundled up in winter clothes, sheltering under Mrs. Harris's big umbrella. Snickers was getting wet (his sweater wasn't waterproof), and Sharon felt sorry for him. In the end, he refused point blank to walk any farther, and Sharon picked him up since Mrs. Harris was holding the umbrella. He had ice stuck between his toes.

In answer to Mrs. Harris's question, Sharon said that she liked Fr. Karimu very much, but he wasn't at all like she had thought he would be.

"Why? What did you think he'd be like?" asked Mrs. Harris.

"Oh, I don't know. Maybe kind of cold and too important to bother with me. But he's so kind and so friendly … I see how he could be everybody's father. He's awfully big, though!"

"And awfully brown?" Mrs. Harris laughed.

"He seemed like he really cared about me," continued Sharon.

They stopped talking for a minute to cross a street, jumping across a big slushy puddle that had built up near the curb.

Mrs. Harris had been considering Sharon's last remark. "That's what the best priests are like," she commented. "Oh, you'll meet a cold, distant priest once in a while, but especially the Tanzanian priests almost never are."

"But I never knew you lived in Ta-zania," Sharon said, reminded of her many questions from the day before. "Tell me about it."

"Tanzania," corrected Mrs. Harris. "I'll tell you about it while we eat our snack. Something hot sounds good today. Would you like some hot chocolate?"

They turned the last corner onto their street, and Mrs. Harris reached over with her free hand to fiddle with one of Snickers's paws, as he lay nestled in Sharon's arms. She was trying to work the lumps of ice out from between his toes with her fingers so that he wouldn't track wetness all over the house. She really needed his towel, and both hands, to finish the job, so, leaving the umbrella outside, she grabbed the towel off its hook on the kitchen wall as they walked in through the back door of the house, instead of the more usual front door, because it was such a wet day. Taking Snickers from Sharon, she soon had his paws dry.

When they were finally seated at the kitchen table with their drinks, Mrs. Harris asked, "What do you want to know?"

Sharon watched Mrs. Harris stirring just one spoonful of sugar into her tea.

"Well, how long did you live there in Tasmania? And when?"

"Tanzania," corrected Mrs. Harris automatically. "Tasmania's different. I lived in Tanzania for close to four years, came back two years ago. Really, I didn't even want to come back, I liked it so much. But the climate was beginning to try me rather badly. You wouldn't

believe how hot and humid it can be there. And no air condition-
ing."

"What were you doing there?" Sharon continued her questioning.

"At first, I just taught English, then I started a school library. I
became the librarian as well as teaching, and I read to the children a
lot."

"Just like you do with me."

"Yes, it's one of my favorite things to do. As you know. And I
always read to my children when they were growing up. Three of
them I read to until they were seventeen."

"Seventeen!" exclaimed Sharon. "They were all grown up. What
did you read them when they were seventeen?"

"Oh, grown-ups' books," answered Mrs. Harris. "I was reading
them mostly grown-ups' books by the time they were thirteen or
fourteen: novels, mysteries, science fiction."

"So, being read to isn't just for little kids?"

"Heavens, no!" Mrs. Harris looked shocked. "I used to read to
my father, too. I did it for the last five or six years of his life. And my
mother and father often read books to each other. People of all ages
like being read to. It has nothing to do with being able to read books
for yourself."

Sharon nodded her head in agreement. "Yeah, it's fun. But, so
you really do speak Swahili, don't you?"

"I can get along in it," admitted Mrs. Harris. "Let's go read."

Chapter 11

The Mass

A few days later, Mrs. Harris took Sharon to Mass at the Cathedral of the Madeleine, where Fr. Karimu was the assistant. Sharon's mother didn't mind her going. She thought church would be an interesting experience for Sharon.

And Sharon *was* interested. She had no idea what it would be like but was curious. By now, she trusted Mrs. Harris enough that as long as she could stay with her she was willing to try this new thing. Sharon had prayed the prayer about God showing her if He was real, but so far nothing had happened, and she was disappointed.

Mrs. Harris had said that it might take a while, but Sharon had hoped God would answer her right away.

"What do I wear for Mass?" she asked Mrs. Harris the Friday before.

"Well, I always wear a dress," replied Mrs. Harris. "It's pretty much the only time that I do, because usually I like pants a lot better. Pants!" She laughed. "I taught British English for too long. They say 'trousers' in Tanzania."

"They do?" asked Sharon, surprised.

"Yes, the word 'pants' seems to mean 'underpants' in Great Britain or in the countries that the British colonized," explained Mrs. Harris. "Anyway, do you have any dresses or skirts?"

"I think I've got one dress," answered Sharon, "unless it's gotten too small. I haven't worn it for a while."

89

"Just wear your best outfit, whatever that is," advised Mrs. Harris. "It's not the most important thing anyway. You'll see people dressed every which way. Americans are awfully informal these days. Some people even wear jeans to Mass. As long as you don't wear jeans, you'll be better dressed than some of the congregation."

On Sunday morning, Sharon went next door to Mrs. Harris's house at 10:15, as they'd arranged. It was a cold, gray day, but happily it wasn't actually raining as they drove downtown to the Cathedral. "I usually like to go to the earlier Mass," Mrs. Harris told Sharon. "The parking is a lot easier than for the eleven o'clock. But you'll get to hear the choir this way."

"Will we see Fr. Karimu?" asked Sharon.

"Oh, yes," replied Mrs. Harris, turning a corner and glancing back over her shoulder as she signaled to move into the left lane. "It's his week for the eleven o'clock."

She found a good parking place by the side of the Cathedral, and they got out of the car. Sharon's dress had proved to be too small, so she was wearing her newest outfit—a birthday present—purple leggings and an oversized sweater of some nubbly material, patterned with large purple flowers on an off-white background. Her winter coat was almost new, too, as she had outgrown her old one the previous winter. Her best shoes were brown half boots. Mrs. Harris thought she looked nice and told her so.

Mrs. Harris, herself, was dressed in a longish skirt and a white blouse, with one of her usual Fair Isle cardigans over it, a wool coat, and the perennial sensible shoes. Her gray hair looked nice, Sharon thought, curly at the ends from an old permanent.

As they walked under the shadow of the tall stone building, Sharon looked up in awe. "It's so big!" she exclaimed.

Mrs. Harris nodded agreement. They turned a corner of the building and saw the courtyard, or plaza, outside the Cathedral, with the fountain, empty for the winter, in the middle. Other buildings, old houses some of them, enclosed two other sides of the courtyard, but it was the Cathedral that dominated it.

In the car, Mrs. Harris had talked to Sharon about what to expect and how to behave. She told Sharon not to mind that people would be standing or kneeling during parts of the Mass—that Sharon should feel free just to watch or to join in, whichever she wanted. "Don't worry about it," she had said. "You just do whatever parts you can or want to. The only thing is not to talk in church. If you absolutely have to ask me a question right then, I'll give you a pen and you can write on the bulletin. That's the paper they'll give us that tells what songs we'll sing and what parts of the Bible we'll hear. But wait till afterward, when we're out of church, to ask questions if you can."

Sharon understood. She was keyed up about being there, but not exactly frightened. Or at least, curiosity was her predominant emotion.

Mrs. Harris led Sharon through a door and down a hallway past an elevator to the vestibule. An usher gave each of them a copy of the bulletin that Mrs. Harris had told Sharon about. They walked through a set of big double doors into the church itself.

It was the smells that Sharon noticed first. She didn't know what she was smelling, but it was different from any place she had ever been. Damp stone? Candles? Wooden pews? The church smelled old, Sharon thought. Her next impression was one of hugeness. She thought she had never been in such a big room. The ceiling was far away, up overhead. It had big lights suspended on long chains at intervals along it. The ceiling itself was arched and, like all of the building, was made of stone.

Sharon gawked while Mrs. Harris dipped her finger into the font of holy water by the door and crossed herself. Then she took Sharon's hand and led her far forward toward the white marble altar. When they arrived at the fifth or sixth pew from the front, Mrs. Harris made a complicated motion, touching her right knee to the ground at the same time that she made the sign of the cross with her right hand, then led Sharon into the pew, where she immediately pulled the kneeler down and knelt on it for a few minutes, praying, Sharon supposed.

Sharon sat next to the aisle on the hard wooden pew, resting her feet on the kneeler, and looking around at everything, big-eyed. She soaked in the atmosphere of the place. It felt hushed and expectant, as more and more people trailed in. More than that, though, Sharon felt for the first time the atmosphere of a place that has been much prayed in. It felt different from any place she had ever been.

She was overwhelmed with so many things to look at. There were big murals all across the front, of bigger-than-life-sized people. One of them was wearing what looked like a leopard skin. There was a woman dressed in a white robe who had a lamb on a leash. The lamb looked a lot like Snickers.

There were angels painted all over the front panels of the ceiling. There were also angels painted as if hanging in the air over the murals of the people. High above the altar was a complicated picture with a bird, an old man with a gray beard, and Jesus on a cross. There were angels in this picture, too.

She stared at Jesus on the cross for a while, then her attention wandered to the beautiful colors of the huge stained-glass windows running down each side of the Cathedral. There were ten or twelve of them and most had dates and names at the bottom. She read such entries as, "In memoriam James W. Miller, Donated by G. B. and P. T. Miller, 1898" and wondered at what a long time ago that was. Almost a hundred years!

A big boy dressed in a white robe appeared near the altar and began to light the candles, one by one. He used a candlelighter, a long metal stick that reminded Sharon of a shepherd's crook, except that it was a little more complicated. There was a flame at its tip. Its length enabled him to reach the candles that were high up. And there were a lot of candles: two on the altar, two groups of six or eight candles on gold-colored stands in front of a strange wooden screen that divided the space behind the altar from an area beyond it that Sharon couldn't see very well.

After he had lit all these candles, he came forward and lighted two candles on a huge Advent wreath, about five feet across, that Sharon hadn't noticed until then. As she looked toward it, she saw beyond it what appeared to be a big nativity set which was off to the left in an alcove. It was on the other side of the church from where she was sitting, so she couldn't see it very well.

After all the candles were lit, the boy walked out. Shortly after that, there was a sort of "whooshing" sound and the lights dimmed, then came back up after a moment or two. Sharon turned to look back to where she thought the sound had come from and saw to her surprise a big balcony high up at the back of the church. It held what looked like hundreds of pipes, ranging from huge ones twelve or fifteen feet high and as big around as tree trunks, down to very little ones. The whooshing sound had come from there. Mrs. Harris had stopped kneeling and now sat beside Sharon on the pew. Sharon looked at her with questioning eyes. Mrs. Harris took a pen and wrote on the edge of her bulletin, "Pipe organ. It draws so much electricity that it makes all the lights go dim when it's turned on."

Music began, and the sound of it filled the church.

Mrs. Harris touched Sharon's arm to get her attention and pointed to the top of the bulletin. The words read, "Prelude - Toccata and Fugue in g minor … Johann Sebastian Bach (1685-1750)." Sharon didn't know what any of that meant, but it started her studying her copy of the bulletin. There were a lot of strange words: Processional hymn, Gloria, Sanctus, Agnus Dei.

While Sharon was still reading the bulletin, puzzling over it, the music came to a stop. Suddenly, a bell rang and there was a noise of shuffling as all the people, hundreds of them by now, stood up. The organ launched into a hymn.

Looking back again, Sharon saw that a big boy, dressed in a long black robe, had rung a brass bell mounted on the back wall of the church. She also saw a lot of people dressed in black and white standing at the back of the church.

Then, the singing began and two boys, Sharon's age or a few years older, walked to the front of the group, each holding a large lighted candle. There was also a white-robed man holding a crucifix like the one on Mrs. Harris's wall. This crucifix, though, was mounted on a pole.

As verse one of the hymn ended, the man lifted the crucifix and began a slow march down the center aisle of the church, flanked by the two boys with candles and followed by the people in black and white, all of whom were singing.

Sharon's heart thrilled at the two columns of people singing and pacing so slowly down the aisle. They were singing in parts, so first the sopranos passed, singing the melody, then other women, but not singing the melody, then men singing something else altogether. All of it harmonized so well, and fitted together so beautifully, that Sharon suddenly felt exalted—the candles, singing, and long lines of people processing in thrilled her to the marrow.

She stood there staring, drinking it all in, her eyes bright. Behind the choir came a man dressed in white with a purple stole that ran diagonally across his chest from his left shoulder to his right hip. He was carrying a book covered in what looked to Sharon like gold. Last of all came Fr. Karimu, dressed entirely in rich purple vestments. He looked magnificent and was singing with a full voice. As he passed Sharon he looked down and smiled at her.

The procession passed, the choir members bowing to the altar two by two then climbing the stairs to the area behind the altar, on the other side of the wooden screen, where they had places to sit. Fr. Karimu bowed to the altar, too, then walked up around the back of it where the other man, having laid down the big gold-covered book was waiting for him. They bent over together, kissed the altar, then went to stand in front of chairs off to one side.

When the song ended, Fr. Karimu made the sign of the cross as he proclaimed, "In the name of the Father, and of the Son, and of the Holy Spirit," and the Mass began.

Of course, Sharon didn't take in half of what was going on, not a quarter of it really. What she did absorb was the atmosphere: the beautiful music and singing in four-part harmony, the intoning and chanted responses of the people around her, all acting as one in reciting the words, all standing or kneeling or sitting in unison.

She didn't understand the words or the concepts behind the words. But she did understand the beauty of it all—the music, the building with its murals, stained-glass windows, marble altar, candles. Her soul soaked it all in like a sponge. She looked up at Mrs. Harris sometimes and saw joy on her face.

When it came time to go forward to receive the Eucharist, Mrs. Harris took Sharon with her, but indicated by signs that Sharon should cross her arms over her chest. Fr. Karimu didn't give Sharon one of the white wafers that he was giving to the others but instead put his hand on her head and said a blessing over her.

Soon after that, it was over, the last prayer said, the blessing given, and the last song sung, during which the crucifix holder, candle bearers, choir, and priest processed out, in the same order as at the beginning of the Mass.

As they left the cathedral, Mrs. Harris stopped to speak to Fr. Karimu, who was standing, still in his vestments, greeting people as they went by. He and Mrs. Harris shook hands. He told Sharon how glad he was that she had come and asked her if she had liked it. She smiled and nodded vigorously. They walked on and were soon outside in the chill December air. She took a breath of it, then preceded Mrs. Harris to the car, hopping and skipping the whole way.

"Well, you seem pretty happy," Mrs. Harris commented as she started the car. "Did you like it?"

"I liked it so much!" said Sharon, struggling for words. "It felt …
it felt … holy, I guess. And all the pictures, and that music thing.
What did you say it was? I never saw a place like that. It was beautiful!"

"I'm glad you liked it," said Mrs. Harris. "'That music thing' is
called a pipe organ."

"And Fr. Karimu smiled at me as he walked by. Did you see
that?"

"No, did he?"

"Yes," said Sharon. "But the only thing is that I don't understand
it. I've got to learn a lot more. My daddy's Catholic, isn't he? I've got
to talk to him."

"That's a good idea," agreed Mrs. Harris.

Chapter 12

Sharon Visits Her Father

That afternoon, as usual on a Sunday, Sharon went with her mom to visit her father. He looked as he always looked these days, tired and thin, with lines of pain etched into his face.

Sharon was too excited, too full of questions about the new things she was learning and the new experience of that morning, to be as upset as usual by her father's appearance.

She started right in, "Daddy, Daddy, I went to church this morning!"

Her mother smiled at the greeting. "You remember we talked about it, Jim? About letting her go to Mass with Mrs. Harris?"

Sharon's father nodded. "Where did she take you, Baby?" he asked.

"We went to the Cathedral, Daddy, downtown, and I heard a pipe organ and Fr. Karimu was there all dressed in purple and, and…"

"Whoa, slow down!" her father interrupted. "Didn't you get bored? You're pretty young to sit through a whole hour of church."

"But there was so much to look at," protested Sharon. "Everyone was saying things all together and standing up and kneeling down at the same time. I don't know how they do that. And there were songs and things, and Fr. Karimu blessed me. You know what, Daddy?"

"No. What?" asked her father.

"You know how when they walk in and they're singing and all dressed up, you know?"

Her father nodded.

"Well, Fr. Karimu was coming last and when he passed me, he smiled at me!"

"Did he?" smiled her father. "What's he like, anyway?"

"He's a Ta-za-nian, Daddy, and he's awfully big and brown but he's really friendly. But he talks funny."

"*What* is he?"

Sharon's mother broke in, "From Tanzania, I think she means. He's from Africa."

"And, Daddy, did you know that Mrs. Harris used to live in Ta-za-nia? She lived there for years and years, and she can talk Swahili besides also French."

"Can she?" asked her father, startled.

"Anyway, Daddy, I just loved going to church. Why don't we go to church?"

"Well, I don't know, Hon. I guess I just got out of the way of it."

At this point, Sharon's mother broke in with a dry laugh, saying, "Jim, do you mind if I let you handle this by yourself? I want to go get a Coke, but I'll come right back."

"No, go ahead, Sweetheart," he replied. "Sharon and I will be fine."

Sharon's mother lifted an eyebrow and gave her husband an amused look, then turned and walked out of the room.

"Do you believe in God, Daddy?" continued Sharon.

"I believe in Him, yes. But I'm afraid I don't know as much about Him as I should."

"But you should find out," said Sharon, earnestly. "'Cause me, I don't know if I believe in Him yet or not, but I'm going to find out. Do you know what Mrs. Harris said?"

"No, what did Mrs. Harris say?" her father asked patiently.

"She said that it's not the most important thing that I believe in God, 'cause the important thing is that God believes in me. Do you understand that, Daddy?"

"Well, no, I don't entirely think I do," confessed her father.

"Me, neither," confided Sharon. "But it makes me feel good inside. I think it makes me feel like maybe it's not what I do but that God will do something ... if He's real," added Sharon.

She squirmed on the chair she was sitting on. "I wish you could meet Fr. Karimu," she said at last. "'Cause—it's not that I think you're going to die or anything, but Mrs. Harris said that when people die they meet God, so don't you think you should find out more about Him, Daddy ... just in case—even though I *know* you're not going to die—but don't you think you should maybe ..." Her voice trailed off.

"He's really nice, Daddy, Fr. Karimu, *really* he is," she added, squirming again. "Even though he put four spoonfuls of sugar in his tea. Did you ever see anyone put four spoonfuls of sugar in their tea?"

Her father held up a hand and she stopped. He studied her for a few seconds, then said, "No, I don't think I ever did. That sounds like too much sugar. You know, Honey, if it's that important to you, I *will* see him. I don't know if it'll do any good, but if it matters to you, I'll do it. I don't mind meeting him. And anyway, I'm kind of curious about him. I never met a 'Ta-za-nian,'" he teased.

"Oh, Daddy!" Sharon rejoined, but she was happy, nonetheless. "I'll ask Mrs. Harris if he can come visit you."

Mrs. Stover came back into the room soon after that, so the talk moved to other things, and Sharon went out to the hallway with her tote bag of books and read until her mom was ready to leave.

Fr. Karimu came to tea again the next Thursday afternoon. Sharon told him how much she had enjoyed coming to church, and his eyes sparkled.

"I love it, too," he agreed.

When Sharon asked him to visit her father in the hospital, and also mentioned that her father had agreed to a visit, he smiled and said that of course he would go, probably the next day.

He wanted to know which hospital and the room number, but for this they had to drag Mrs. Harris into it, as Sharon simply didn't know. Sharon left the task of arranging a visit to the grown-ups. She was just happy that it was going to happen.

When the time came to go home, she bounced across the yard and announced the good news to her mother. "Mama, Mama, guess what! Fr. Karimu is going to go see Daddy at the hospital!"

Her mother was lukewarm about the idea and didn't seem to think it mattered much either way, but Sharon's joy was unrestrained.

Things were going pretty well at home for her these days, and she was learning to be a bigger help to her mom. Mrs. Stover had only worked part-time before her husband's illness. The next weekend after Sharon had cleaned her room up so nicely, and after she and Mrs. Harris had had another session with the books, Sharon had set to work reorganizing her room, according to the directions given in both books. The new bookcase made a difference and took care of Sharon's small collection of her own books, and the current library books, with room on top for some glass animals, figurines and other little decorative objects. There was an extra shelf where Sharon put her jigsaw puzzles and games.

She also cleaned out her closet and the toy box. Her mother helped her with clothes. They gave outgrown garments to Goodwill, as well as some of the toys that were now too young for Sharon. Some clothing got thrown away if it was truly worn out and was unsuitable for being made into cleaning rags.

What remained of the clothes Sharon put neatly in drawers or on hangers. And she started making better use of the laundry hamper.

The toys now fitted nicely into the toy box. She found boxes and other containers for those toys with small pieces. Altogether, Sharon's room was looking much better these days. After a talk with Mrs. Harris about what needed doing, Sharon took to cleaning her room every Saturday morning, using the first book's method of putting everything on the bed first, then dusting, vacuuming, and putting everything away. But really, it wasn't anywhere near as much work as the first time had been, now that things were better organized.

She began to branch out, too, and spent some time every Saturday picking up the living room after she finished her room. She and her mother made a place in the garage for old newspapers, and the whole house began to look neater on a more regular basis instead of going from clean to disaster and back again over and over.

Mrs. Stover appreciated the help, and told Sharon so. Meals were still pretty much snatch and grab, but there wasn't much Sharon could do about that as she was really a little too young to be using a stove or oven and, of course, she was scared of them both as well.

Mrs. Harris noticed that Sharon seemed to have gained some self-confidence, apparently just from knowing that she could keep her room tidy.

Sharon never knew much about what happened during Fr. Karimu's visit to her dad. True, her dad said that he had enjoyed meeting Fr. Karimu and that they had had a good talk, but he didn't go into any great amount of detail. Certain results of the visit were apparent to Sharon, however. Her father was now a "practicing" Catholic, to the extent that it's possible to be one from a hospital bed. And he apologized to Sharon for not having had her baptized as an infant and told her he'd like her to be baptized as soon as possible. Sharon's mother didn't seem very enthusiastic about the whole thing, but she didn't actually make any objection to it since the idea evidently cheered Sharon's father up.

Mrs. Harris and Sharon had a talk one day at snack about what Mrs. Harris expressed as, "A cradle Catholic is never more than one good confession away from being a Catholic in good standing." First, she had to explain that a "cradle Catholic" meant someone born into a Catholic family, as opposed to a convert, which was what

Mrs. Harris herself was. She had not been a Catholic until she was more than 40 years old. Sharon was surprised.

"I was a Christian from the age of 20, though," Mrs. Harris added, "just not a Catholic."

She further explained that a cradle Catholic isn't usually more than one good confession away from being in good standing because of being "sacramentalized."

"What's that?" asked Sharon.

"Well, it means that they've received the sacraments."

"Sacraments?"

"Sacraments are the way that God usually works in people's lives to draw them closer to Himself. There are seven."

"There are?"

"Nobody has all seven. Let me see if I can name them. I usually come up with six and have to look up the seventh. Baptism is the first sacrament. Your dad's been baptized, of course, and that's only ever done once because it marks your soul indelibly. Like, have you ever seen the word 'indelible' on markers or pens? 'Indelible ink' is the usual term."

Sharon thought about it. "I'm not sure. Maybe."

"It means it won't wash out. We don't give real markers with indelible ink to small children—just water-based ones."

"I've seen 'water-based' written on boxes of markers," put in Sharon.

"Right. Well, baptism makes an indelible mark on your soul that God always sees. Confirmation does that, too. That can be number two. That's the sacrament that says you're grown up and gives you the Holy Spirit so you can be a warrior for Christ. I think the other indelible one is holy orders—becoming a priest. That's our number three. Once a priest, always a priest, in the sense at least that the mark of it can't be erased. Of course, your dad's been confirmed, or I bet he has anyway, but he hasn't been given holy orders."

"'Cause he's not a priest," suggested Sharon.

"Right."

"That's three," said Sharon. "What else?"

"Let me think," said Mrs. Harris. "Communion is number four. Your dad probably made his first Communion when he was seven or eight years old. So, he's had that one. And matrimony is a sacrament if it's done right. Marriage," she added at Sharon's questioning look. "Number five. Two more," she muttered.

"Number six is going to confession, which of course your dad's done. Children make their first confessions around the same time that they make their first Communions. That's partly because the Church doesn't consider that a child can have any actual sins (besides original sin which we're all born with) until the 'age of reason,' as it's called. And that's at about seven years old."

"You mean a little child can't sin? That's weird," said Sharon.

"They can do bad things," Mrs. Harris admitted. "But it wouldn't really be sin. It would be more the fault of grown-ups for not keeping a better eye on them. A baby doesn't have any sense or judgment, right? So, the Church says that, at least on the average, seven might be a pretty good age to start holding people responsible. Of course, they'd still have to be taught right from wrong…"

"Wow!" said Sharon. "That's a lot. So, what's number seven?"

"Got it!" said Mrs. Harris. "Number seven is called 'anointing of the sick' or 'last rites,' or various other names. It's what the priest gives someone who's in danger of death. Goodness! That's enough for one day. Let's get to reading. We won't have much time. But you see what I mean. Your dad's been baptized and several other things, so the most he would need to do is go to confession, and he's back in good standing."

"He can't go anywhere," objected Sharon.

"That's what Catholics say, but they really just mean confessing your sins to a priest, and the priest can come to you," explained Mrs. Harris.

They had started moving toward the living room.

"Let me just go move the Wise Men real quick. I'll be right back," said Sharon.

"Sure," replied Mrs. Harris as Sharon tore off.

Chapter 13

Baptism?

Sharon's dad came home again, but this time he lasted only a week at home. Sharon didn't get excited this time. "Mom was talking about re-, re-…" she said.

"Remission," suggested Mrs. Harris.

"Yeah, I think so," Sharon agreed. "He looks awful sick to me, though. He used to be really big…" She shook her head sadly. When her dad was hospitalized again after only a week, Sharon was almost relieved.

"I know he's disappointed 'cause he wanted to be home for Christmas. I'm disappointed, too, but I think it's easier for him at the hospital. I mean, they can do everything for him there. Of course, he wanted to be with us, and I do see more of him when he's home, but not that much more, if you know what I mean." She looked up at Mrs. Harris. "Mostly he's just in the bedroom resting, or people are helping him with stuff."

Fr. Karimu was coming for tea again, even though it was the week before Christmas. Mrs. Harris explained that he was coming so regularly for Sharon's sake, "barring unforeseen events," she added. "A priest's time is never his own."

They always had the special "Tanzanian tea" on days when he was expected, and Sharon loved it. She tried papayas again, and mangoes, deciding that she liked them both. Hot water and hot milk in thermoses intrigued her, too, and once she tried drinking tea, though Mrs. Harris insisted on putting more milk than tea into her cup. She believed that "cambric tea," as she called it, was more suitable for someone who was still growing.

Mrs. Harris and Sharon, with Snickers, of course, walked home from school quickly in order to get enough reading time in before Fr. Karimu arrived. They started as soon as they got back to Mrs. Harris's house, only taking time for Sharon to move the Wise Men and camels, which were now in the kitchen on their way to the living room mantel. Their regular custom had become reading on the sofa, Sharon on Mrs. Harris' left and Snickers on Sharon's left (or on her lap). That way Sharon could look at the pictures, if any, or Mrs. Harris could point out interesting words or spellings.

When Fr. Karimu arrived, they moved into the kitchen for tea and talk. Sharon lit three candles on the Advent wreath. She had gotten pretty good at it, though she had to use a second match on candle three. The first one had burned too far down. Lighting a match didn't scare her much anymore.

Over tea, Fr. Karimu explained that, although Sharon's father was in a hurry for her to be baptized, there were some things that Sharon needed to learn before that could happen. He had decided to ask the bishop for permission to baptize Sharon in her father's hospital room because that was what her father wanted. This wasn't the usual way, he pointed out, and he wasn't sure if the bishop would okay it or not. Also, it was so close to Christmas that although he would make the request now, he didn't expect to hear back before the New Year. That gave them some time in which to work.

The more normal thing to do with a nine-year-old would be for her to join preparation classes for first Communion, then be baptized as well as making her first Communion with the rest of the class. Classes had started at the end of August at the Cathedral, however, so they had already been going on for several months. More than that, the children being prepared to make their first Communions were only in the second grade, a couple of years younger than Sharon. Luckily, Sharon was young enough that he could justify baptizing her without making her go through a whole series of classes. Fr. Karimu was offering to teach Sharon what she needed to know himself. Then, if she was baptized early, she could make her first Confession and first Communion in May with the second graders. Maybe Mama Wilma would help, he suggested.

Mrs. Harris agreed to help, of course. She assured Fr. Karimu that Sharon was a good student and could probably learn very quickly.

"Are you willing to work?" Fr. Karimu asked her.

Sharon nodded.

"Well, then, I will help you," said Fr. Karimu. "When people go to classes for first Communion it can take nine months, but I am sure you can do it faster with private tuition."

"What's that?" asked Sharon, looking confused.

"Tuition? It means teaching," answered Fr. Karimu.

He looked at Mrs. Harris. "Mama Wilma is an English teacher," he reminded Sharon.

"'Teaching' is right," she said. "That's true. Or 'instruction' or 'tutoring.' At least, that's what it means in British English. But in this country, it more often means how much money you pay for school-ing."

"Yeah," said Sharon. "My mom used to talk about paying tuition when she went to school to learn to be a secretary. That's why I didn't get it. The only time I heard that word before it meant paying money."

"I am not talking about money," Fr. Karimu reassured her. "And you only need to learn some basic facts before being baptized."

Sharon asked, "What do I need to learn?"

"As we are probably doing this in two parts," said Fr. Karimu, "I have written a short list of prayers to learn and ideas to understand in case I get permission to baptize you soon. I will give it to Mama Wilma. Also, I have brought a book." He picked up his briefcase and, opening it, took from it a piece of paper and a small blue book with a picture on the front cover that Sharon found intriguing. The book he handed to Sharon, the piece of paper to Mrs. Harris.

"What's on your paper?" Sharon asked Mrs. Harris.

Mrs. Harris studied the paper. "It's a list. The Our Father, the Hail Mary, and the Glory Be. Those are prayers," she said to Sharon. "Then there are three questions that we'll need to talk about: one about the love of God, one about what sin is, and finally, one about the difference between the Eucharist and bread."

"Right," said Fr. Karimu. "Do you already know any of the pray-ers?" he asked Sharon.

"No, Father," answered Sharon shyly. It was the first time she had called him "Father," but she had heard Mrs. Harris do it pretty often, so she knew it was the right way to address him.

"Well, then," said Fr. Karimu, smiling at Sharon, "you have some work to do."

Sharon looked at the book in her hand. The cover showed a row of children at church, being given communion by Jesus, who was dressed in vestments, like a priest, and who was surrounded by a crowd of people with halos over their heads.

Fr. Karimu leaned across the table and took the book from Sharon, opened the cover, and turned it toward her, then handed it back.

"You see, the book is called the *First Communion Catechism*. These are the basic prayers: the 'Our Father,' the 'Hail Mary,' the 'Glory Be.'" He pointed to them.

"What's a catechism?" asked Sharon.

Fr. Karimu looked at Mrs. Harris, who said, "I think a definition would be that it's a manual for giving religious instruction. Something like that."

"Thank you," Fr. Karimu nodded. "So, you don't already know any of these prayers?" he asked again, as Sharon looked over the first few pages of the book.

Sharon shook her head. "I don't think so. Mrs. Harris told me the sacraments a few days ago though." She grinned at Mrs. Harris as she added, "She remembered all seven!"

Mrs. Harris looked up quickly and smiled at the tease. "Yes, I did," she agreed. "Against all probability. I told Sharon I usually have to search my mind pretty hard for the seventh."

"Today, let us talk about baptism since you might be baptized soon." He flipped through the book. "What did Mama Wilma tell you that a sacrament is?"

Sharon searched her memory. "I think she said they're the way God usually gets nearer to people." She looked questioningly at Mrs. Harris, who nodded.

"Yes," Fr. Karimu agreed. He quoted from the little book, "'A sacrament is an outward sign, instituted by Christ to give 'grace.' Meaning, they are Christ's idea, and he started them. What's 'grace,' do you know?"

Sharon shook her head no.

"Well, we usually say that it is 'unmerited divine assistance.' 'Unmerited' means you don't get help because you deserve it or earn it, but just because God, in His generosity, wants to give it to you."

"Why would He do that?"

"It is hard for us to understand or believe how much God loves us. You can spend your whole life learning to believe that."

Mrs. Harris commented, "So my understanding is that the main thing baptism does is to wash away original sin, and any actual sins, and to 'transfer us from the kingdom of darkness to the kingdom of light,' as the Bible says. In other words, God adopts us as his children. In the ancient Hebrew world, adopted children were treated exactly the same as birth children—or so I've read."

"Is that so?" Fr. Karimu was interested. "Well, that's what baptism is, and that's enough serious talk for one day. Work with Mama Wilma on the list that I gave her, and we will come back to it. You may have the little book for your own." He reached for the thermos to pour himself water for another cup of tea.

Sharon's eyes shone with pleasure at the gift.

In the days that followed, she studied hard to master the contents of Fr. Karimu's list. They talked a little, or Mrs. Harris heard her recite every day during their snack time before they moved to the living room for reading.

Sharon had a talk with Mrs. Harris one day, though, about something that was bothering her.

"Do you ever feel like things are moving too fast?"

"Are you worried about the baptism?" asked Mrs. Harris.

"Yeah, 'cause it could happen so soon, and I *still* don't know if I believe in God—not really."

"Well, let's think about it," said Mrs. Harris soothingly. "Things have changed a little, haven't they? I mean, because your dad wants you to be baptized, right?"

"Right," said Sharon, rather doubtfully.

"So, there's more here than meets the eye just at first. If you were a baby, your parents would decide to get you baptized and work with the Church, and then they'd make promises for you—so would your godparents—and that would be that. You wouldn't have any choice."

"Uh-huh," Sharon agreed. "What kind of promises?"

"To renounce the devil and to teach you the Christian faith. Those are the ones that come to mind at the moment."

"Oh." Sharon sat for a moment thinking about that.

"And if you were a grown-up, nobody would baptize you unless you asked to be baptized. You'd have to start going to Church and learn things and finally be baptized. In the early days of the Church, two thousand years ago, it sometimes took as much as three years, but these days I don't think it ever takes more than about nine months."

"Three years!" exclaimed Sharon. "Wow! Anyway, I'm not a grown-up."

Mrs. Harris nodded in turn. "You're sort of an in-between case. Not a baby but not a grown-up either. So, one thing is that your dad wants you to be baptized. He's even praying for it, Fr. Karimu told me."

"He is?" Sharon's eyes widened. "I didn't know that."

"It will please your father if you're baptized."

"That's what Mama says," Sharon put in. "She says I should just do it to please Daddy. But that seems wrong to me."

"Your conscience would be happier if you knew you believed?" asked Mrs. Harris.

"Yeah, I guess."

"There's another angle, which is that children are supposed to do what their parents want them to, as long as their parents don't want them to do something wrong. It's a virtue," Mrs. Harris said. "A virtue is the opposite of a sin—it's a good thing as opposed to a bad one," she explained, seeing the question in Sharon's eyes. "It's all too seldom observed in this modern age," she added, "but there it is. So, you have a duty, really."

"Hmm." Sharon thought about that. "It's not that I don't want to be baptized. I mean, I still think if that's what makes you feel so safe ... but I just wish I knew..."

"I think you need to go through with it, Sharon. You're right—it is a big event, but it's not totally under your control anymore. And, of course, God *is* going to show Himself to you—I know He is—but

He always does these things in His own time. Getting baptized is not a bad thing to do, your father wants you to be baptized, and you'd be obeying him."

Sharon nodded thoughtfully.

"Just speak to your conscience," Mrs. Harris advised. "Tell it you're doing what your dad wants and you're obeying your parents, and it needs to simmer down." She smiled.

"That's what I used to tell my children once in a while when they got too loud in the car. 'Simmer down back there!'" she barked. "I think my Mom used to say it when my brothers and I were children. Just speak to your conscience." She laughed.

"Simmer down!" said Sharon experimentally and laughed, too.

Fr. Karimu and Mrs. Harris had explained the basics of the faith to Sharon, and she had taken it all in, but she was still holding a big mental reservation. Was it really all true? Did God exist? It made it seem more likely to her as she spent time with grown-ups who clearly thought God did exist and lived by it. She hoped God would answer her prayer soon if He really existed.

So, she still wasn't sure if she believed in God, but she had decided that God and the Church were the reasons why Mrs. Harris seemed so peaceful and secure, and she wanted to be that way, too.

When she thought of Mrs. Harris, it was as though she saw a light in her mind, as though Mrs. Harris's love was shining, not in real life, but in Sharon's mind. Christianity, too, was beginning to loom large in her mind, like a bulwark or a rampart. Sharon didn't know either of those words, but that's what she saw when she thought of the Church, a "mighty fortress," shaped like a ship, standing on a hill. Mrs. Harris and Fr. Karimu were standing on top of the high wall, at its prow, but Sharon herself was down on the grass which surrounded the fortress and didn't know how to get in. Maybe this was the way. Maybe mastering the contents of the booklet and being baptized and receiving first Communion would put her up on the rampart with them.

She still didn't know for sure if she believed in God, but it was beginning to seem more and more possible that He existed. If she could just find Him!

Chapter 14

Getting Ready for Christmas

Sharon and Mrs. Harris had another discussion about faith one day as they walked home from Sharon's school. Sharon started the discussion by sighing as she said, "I just don't know how to *find* God."

Mrs. Harris smiled. "Yes, but here's the thing of it: it's not really a matter of looking around, as though you'll come upon Him somewhere. Think about this: God is existence itself. God *is*."

Sharon frowned. "He *is?*" she asked.

"In Him we live and move, and have our being," said Mrs. Harris. "That's from the Bible. When Moses asked God for His name, God answered 'I am' or 'I am who am,' depending on whose translation you're using."

"Oh, I don't understand that at all!" Sharon exclaimed.

"It's hard to wrap your mind around. You know, in an odd way I think that makes the idea more believable," replied Mrs. Harris. "If religion were something people had invented, we probably could understand it completely. If you see what I mean," she added.

"God is higher than we are. That's why there are things that we couldn't know on our own. God has to reveal Himself to us. How well does Snickers understand me?" Mrs. Harris asked.

"Snickers?" Sharon laughed. She was beginning to get it.

"Snickers," confirmed Mrs. Harris. "People are higher beings than dogs. Snickers knows a lot about me, in a way. He's been with me for almost ten years. He knows my daily routine: when he'll get fed, when walks are likely to happen. I think he even knows when I'm happy, or sad, or angry. But he knows nothing at all about my study of linguistics or what I'm doing when I pray. It doesn't mean anything to him that I do a crossword puzzle. He can't understand all of me because I'm a higher being than he is."

"Yeah, he just knows the simple stuff," Sharon agreed.

"And at that, maybe he knows more about me than I know about God. God made everything—stars, galaxies, planets—everything. Sometimes, I think that us trying to understand God is more like goldfish trying to understand people. How much does a goldfish know? Well, maybe that's too pessimistic. But don't go scouting around for God; we're *in* Him."

Sharon nodded thoughtfully.

Another day they talked about time on their way home from school. Mrs. Harris explained that God's timing is one of the hardest things for people to understand. God is never in a hurry, and He knows the end from the beginning. We're the ones who get in a hurry. The Bible says that 'one day for the Lord is as a thousand years and a thousand years is as one day.'"

"What does that mean, do you think?" asked Sharon.

"It's hard to explain and hard for grown-ups to understand, much less little girls. I've been working on understanding it for much of my life. But roughly it's like this: God is *outside* of time. That's what eternity means. It doesn't mean that something goes on forever, although we often use it that way. Really, though, it means that time is something God created, too. But imagining living without time is just about impossible, isn't it?"

Sharon tried to imagine it and couldn't.

"You *have* to have time!" she exclaimed.

"Yes, that's the way it seems to us now, but I suppose that's because we're *in* time. Like a fish in water trying to imagine breathing without water. If fish could imagine. Which they can't," she added.

Sharon was silent as they finished the walk home. It was too hard for her to understand how anything could be without time, but she was a little comforted by Mrs. Harris's confidence that an answer to her question about the existence of God would be forthcoming.

Christmas was just days away. The Wise Men and camels were in the living room now, on their way to visit the Christ Child. They processed all around the room, from bookshelf to bookshelf.

Mrs. Harris and Sharon were reading another Rumer Godden book. This one was called *The Kitchen Madonna*, about a little boy trying to make an icon for the family's Ukrainian servant who was homesick for the things of her childhood. In making the icon, he came out of his shell, so to speak, and became a more loving member of his family. It wasn't, strictly speaking, a Christmas story, but it *was* a wonderful story to read at Christmas time.

Mrs. Harris had a well-worn copy of a book based on Clement Moore's poem "A Visit from Saint Nicholas," the poem that starts out "'Twas the Night Before Christmas." The illustrator of Mrs. Harris's copy of the book was the same artist who had drawn the pictures for *The Tawny, Scrawny Lion* and a number of other well-known Little Golden books. This book was the actual one that Mrs. Harris had grown up with herself, besides raising her children on it, so it wasn't in very good shape, but was still readable. Sometimes, she read it to Sharon before the other reading of the day began.

After *The Kitchen Madonna,* Mrs. Harris began to read a real Christmas story, *The Lion in the Box* by Marguerite de Angeli. It was short, and they got through it in two days. The story was about a destitute widow and her family of five children living in New York City in the early 1900's. According to the author, the story was substantially true, not really fiction. Sharon was bothered by the poverty portrayed in the book.

Mrs. Harris reassured her, pointing out that many people had been very much poorer a hundred years before. "Are you worried for yourself?" she asked.

"I suppose so, maybe partly," Sharon answered.

"Things are different today," reiterated Mrs. Harris. "And there's only one of you. This woman had five children."

The magic of the story consisted in the big wooden crate, almost too big to fit through the doorway, that was delivered on Christmas Eve to the children, their mother being at work. The man who brought it upstairs to the family's tenement threatened that there was "a lion in the box" so that the children wouldn't try to open it before their mother got back from work. The children were scared almost into fits.

After their mother finally arrived home and calmed the children down, they all went to sleep, then opened the large crate on Christmas morning. It was found to contain a wonderful assortment of food, clothing, and toys, sent by a rich woman whom the mother had met while cleaning an office.

The description of each item, culminating in a large, well-furnished doll house and its accompanying toy farm made the book exciting, as did the afterword, which spoke of what the children did when they grew up.

In *The Lion in the Box,* the story of Christmas was mentioned as one that the girls loved. Mrs. Harris stopped reading as a thought struck her.

"I bet you've never heard that story, have you?" she asked Sharon. "It's in the Bible."

"No, I haven't," agreed Sharon. "Is it really in the Bible?"

"In the Gospel of St. Luke. Do you remember what the gospels are?"

"Matthew, Mark, Luke, John, bless the bed that I lie on. That's how you remember them, right? Didn't you say they're the first four books of the Bible and they talk about Jesus?"

"The first four books of the New Testament, yes. Let me read the story to you. It won't take long."

Sharon nodded agreement as Mrs. Harris walked over to one of the bookcases and pulled out a beautiful leather-bound Bible with what looked like gold-edged pages. The pages were very thin, too, Sharon noticed as Mrs. Harris flipped through the book.

This Bible is called the King James Version. It's an early translation into English, and the English is old-fashioned and beautiful. From the year 1611, imagine! So don't try to understand every word. Just let the words wash over you, and you'll get the gist of it. It's Saint Luke, chapter 2, the first 20 verses."

She began to read,

"And it came to pass in those days, that there went out a de-
cree from Cæsar Augustus, that all the world should be
taxed.

(And this taxing was first made when Cyrenius was governor
of Syria.) And all went to be taxed, every one into his own
city.

And Joseph also went up from Galilee, out of the city of Naz-
areth, into Judæa, unto the city of David, which is called
Bethlehem (because he was of the house and lineage of
David): to be taxed with Mary his espoused wife, being
great with child.

And so it was, that, while they were there, the days were ac-
complished that she should be delivered.

And she brought forth her firstborn son, and wrapped him
in swaddling clothes, and laid him in a manger; because
there was no room for them in the inn.

And there were in the same country shepherds abiding in the
field, keeping watch over their flock by night.

And, lo, the angel of the Lord came upon them, and the glory
of the Lord shone round about them; and they were sore
afraid.

And the angel said unto them, Fear not: for, behold, I bring
you tidings of great joy, which shall be to all people.

For unto you is born this day in the city of David a Saviour,
which is Christ the Lord.

And this shall be a sign unto you: Ye shall find the babe
wrapped in swaddling clothes, lying in a manger.

And suddenly there was with the angel a multitude of the
heavenly host praising God, and saying,

Glory to God in the highest, and on earth peace, good will
toward men.

And it came to pass, as the angels were gone away from them
into heaven, the shepherds said one to another, Let us
now go even unto Bethlehem, and see this thing which is
come to pass, which the Lord hath made known unto us.

And they came with haste, and found Mary, and Joseph, and
the babe lying in a manger.

And when they had seen it, they made known abroad the
saying which was told them concerning this child.

And all they that heard it wondered at those things which
were told them by the shepherds.

But Mary kept all these things, and pondered them in her
heart.

And the shepherds returned, glorifying and praising God for
all the things that they had heard and seen, as it was told
unto them."

"So that's why there are shepherds," Sharon commented, looking over at the nativity set on the mantel.

"Right, though I don't suppose they really had any sheep with
them, like in the nativity sets" answered Mrs. Harris. "Sheep don't
move very fast. You couldn't possibly 'come with haste' if sheep were
involved."

"It's really beautiful," said Sharon. "I think I got most of it. Read
it again." Mrs. Harris read it again. This time Sharon moved closer

and watched the words as they were being read. Then they went on with *The Lion in the Box,* which was getting more and more exciting.

As with Thanksgiving Day, Christmas this year was not a happy time for Sharon. With her father in the hospital, there could be no going away to visit relatives. Sharon's mother couldn't bring herself to do any Christmas shopping and wouldn't have had the time or money to do much in any case.

Worst of all, Mrs. Harris went to spend Christmas with her children in California. She would be gone a whole week. She had been intending to put Snickers in a kennel, but Sharon asked if she could dog sit. After some reluctance on the part of Sharon's mother, this was agreed to. After all, Sharon would be out of school the whole time that Mrs. Harris would be gone, so she would have plenty of time to spend with the little dog, who would not need to be left alone in the house for long periods of time.

And Sharon's mother was going to be allowed to take the whole week off work by using a couple of her vacation days in addition to the normal time off for Christmas that everybody got. Mrs. Harris pointed out that having Snickers might even enable Mrs. Stover to leave Sharon home alone for limited periods of time, as the dog would be a reassuring presence. "If Snickers isn't barking, then there simply isn't anything going on," as Mrs. Harris put it.

Mrs. Harris was leaving on a plane the evening of the last day of school. They had one last day of her watching Sharon. Already, the house looked different to Sharon, though Mrs. Harris hadn't yet left.

The first thing they did when they arrived after school was for Sharon to help Mrs. Harris by kneeling down and snapping the latches on a big suitcase while Mrs. Harris sat on it.

This made Mrs. Harris laugh, and she quoted something from a book that she hadn't yet read to Sharon: "'There's two advantages to being stout. One, you can shut suitcases with your weight alone and, two, it takes a lot to sweep you off your feet.' That's from a book by Elizabeth Enright. I'll have to read it to you one of these days. It's a good book. Anyway, it sure helps to have someone else to fasten the latches. Thank you."

They had their usual snack, but Sharon noticed that the refrigerator was much emptier than usual, and the house already felt lonely to her. It looked barer than usual, too, because things were missing from their usual places, including the Advent wreath.

Yesterday, all four candles had been lit. Sharon had particularly admired the spiral effect given by the candles being of different lengths. The candle that had been lit during the first week was shorter than the candle that hadn't been lit until the second week. It in turn was shorter than the pink candle and the last candle was still almost new. Now, the wreath was missing.

Sharon asked Mrs. Harris about it, and Mrs. Harris looked a little embarrassed. "Well, I'm taking it to California," she admitted, after clearing her throat. "I've got it in a box in my big suitcase. That's probably why the suitcase was so hard to close. It takes up far too much room. It's silly, really," she continued. "But I didn't want to do without it. My children always loved having them, but we're not meeting at anyone's house, just having Christmas at a rented cabin on the beach, so I'm afraid there won't be a wreath unless I bring one."

On this last day, some of their time together was spent going over what Sharon would need to do for Snickers. Mrs. Harris had written a sheet of instructions about feeding, brushing, and walking him. She pointed out that Sharon would need to pick up dog poop from the yard at least every other day. And she recommended that Sharon put some baggies in the pocket of her winter coat whenever she took Snickers for his daily walk, so that she could pick up any droppings produced on the walk.

"I know," she laughed, as Sharon wrinkled her nose. "But other people really hate it when dogs poop in their yard. And I don't blame them, do you? You've been watching me do it all along. It's not that bad, Sharon."

Mrs. Harris managed to fit all of Snickers's paraphernalia into a paper grocery bag with handles. Besides a box of baggies, there was a small bag of dog food, a food bowl, a water bowl, a box of dog biscuits, Snickers's brush, a towel for drying wet or icy feet, and a selection of dog sweaters. Sharon planned that Snickers would sleep on her bed, and Mrs. Stover had agreed, so the dog bed was left behind.

After reading an assortment of picture books involving Christmas, Mrs. Harris gave Sharon two things. One was a Christmas present. It was a box, heavy for its size of six or eight inches square, beautifully wrapped in shiny paper which had a pattern of holly leaves all over it and with a crimson bow which matched the color of the holly berries. The second thing was a small card with Fr. Karimu's address and phone number on it. "Just in case you need anything," Mrs. Harris said.

Mrs. Harris carried Snickers and the grocery bag of his supplies and accompanied Sharon across the yard to the door of her house. Sharon had about all she could do carrying her Christmas present with both hands. Once inside the door, she put it down on the sofa, took the bag of Snickers's belongings and put it next to the present, then took the leash from Mrs. Harris. Sharon's mom and Mrs. Harris chatted for a few minutes, exchanging Christmas greetings, then Mrs. Harris gave Sharon a big hug and wished her a Merry Christmas.

"I'll see you in a week," she promised. "Then the Wise Men can finish their journey to the crèche." She patted Snickers and was gone.

Chapter 15

Christmas

It was a good thing that Sharon had Snickers. He brightened her Christmas, which would have been a dreary one, otherwise. There were only two other spots of light for her: Christmas Eve Mass and Mrs. Harris's Christmas present. And Sharon almost didn't get to go to Mass on Christmas Eve.

She hadn't supposed that she would use the card with Fr. Karimu's phone number on it, but she did. The problem was that Sharon's mother didn't want to take her to Mass. She said she had enough to do without sitting and being bored for an hour, "or very likely more." They argued about it. Sharon could be stubborn when she really wanted a thing. In the end, Mrs. Stover suggested angrily that Sharon should call "that priest," and maybe *he* would take her to church if she wanted to go so badly.

Sharon was frightened of using the telephone and brooded in her room for an hour or more. Snickers was nice to have around at a time like this. He just sat on her lap while she sulked. He was warm and fuzzy and comforting to hug.

Learning to clean her room and lighting the Advent wreath every day had helped Sharon feel more confident. She had begun to see that it was possible to fight against her fears. So, now she worked up her courage and called the number on the card Mrs. Harris had given her. She was soon speaking with Fr. Karimu. He was friendly and offered to come for her when he heard her mother was reluctant.

He would take her to the children's Mass at 6:30 and would pick her up at 5:30, which would leave him enough time to vest before Mass. Sharon's mother couldn't very well protest, having made the suggestion herself, so it was agreed.

Sharon was waiting excitedly when Fr. Karimu drove up and came to the front door. Mrs. Stover hadn't met him before. And he seemed to intimidate her, being so large and foreign. He took her hand and held it for a minute, which she also found strange, while he introduced himself. His manner was serious, but she noticed how knowing his eyes were, as if he saw all the hard parts of her life and sympathized with her. She even admitted to Sharon, afterwards, that she could see why Sharon liked him so much.

At the Cathedral, Fr. Karimu took good care of Sharon. He found her a seat in the first pew, "where I can keep an eye on you," as he said. She sat with a big family that Fr. Karimu knew. They made her welcome and put her next to the mother and baby, with several of the family's children on her other side.

Sharon hadn't sat so far forward when she came with Mrs. Harris. She was delighted to be on the other side of the main aisle where she had a good view of the huge manger scene that she had glimpsed before. The baby Jesus was in the manger. Real straw was strewn all over the floor. The figures were life-sized and were particularly beautiful. Their clothes were brightly painted, and the expressions on their faces were realistic. The donkey looked sweet, too, Sharon thought. Sharon spent the time until Mass started looking at the scene and wondering what it would have been like to be present at Christ's birth.

The church was wonderfully decorated. There were dozens of poinsettias scattered around the altar and by the side chapels. Bunches of evergreens were tied to the ends of the pews and fastened high up on the walls, between the stained glass windows. There was even a Christmas tree, tall and majestic, and covered with little gold lights, sitting in the chapel on the other side of the aisle.

And the candles! Someone had set up extra candle stands, each bearing ten or twelve candles. It took the altar boy quite a while to get all of them lit. Everything made of cloth was white with gold trim—the altar cloths and the cloth over the lectern. When Fr. Karimu processed in behind the altar servers and choir, Sharon saw that his vestments were made of a magnificent shiny gold cloth of a sort that she had never seen before.

The Mass was a little chaotic and noisy. There were so many children! The Cathedral's children's choir sang the Mass, which seemed just right for a children's Mass. They sang a lot of the best Christmas carols. Sharon enjoyed every moment, though she felt a bit lonely to be there without anyone she knew.

After Mass she found Fr. Karimu and stood next to him while he shook people's hands and wished them a Merry Christmas. Then, he took her back to the sacristy, where she had never been before, while he unvested. There were quite a few people there, putting things away and hanging up robes. It was a room with a table, lots of cabinets, and several wardrobes. Fr. Karimu showed her where the chalices and other things were kept. She was especially interested in all the vestments hanging up in the wardrobes. The church had so many of them, in different sizes and colors, all of them clean and pressed, looking very beautiful.

When she got home, she had a snack, then it was time for bed.

On Christmas Day, Snickers woke Sharon up by pawing at her and snuffling in her face. He wanted to go out. Sharon got up and let him out into the fenced back yard. Her mom wasn't up. It didn't seem as though there was even going to be Christmas this year, really. Sharon hadn't hung up a Christmas stocking, and her mom hadn't brought up the subject. They didn't have a tree. The house wasn't decorated in any way.

Sharon got herself a glass of orange juice and a bowl of cereal. After she let Snickers back in and fed him—he hadn't wanted to stay out long in the cold—she ate the cereal and drank her juice.

Then she decided to open Mrs. Harris's present. It was a set of paperback books, a beautiful edition of all seven of C. S. Lewis's Narnia books in a box. The magnificence of the present almost took Sharon's breath away. She was used to getting smaller presents, or at least useful ones like new clothes.

It also represented a concession on Mrs. Harris's part. Sharon had been wanting to hear the Narnia books, having been attracted by the title of one, *The Horse and His Boy*, which seemed entirely backwards to her. A boy might have a horse. Horses didn't have boys. Mrs. Harris had thought that Sharon was a bit young for the Narnia books, that there was no point in rushing things, and that there were lots of other good books, too. Sharon figured that if Mrs. Harris had given her the books it meant that she was now willing to read them to her.

Later in the day, when Sharon's mother finally got up and they went to visit her dad, Sharon took the books along, both because she wanted to show them to her father and because she couldn't bear to be parted from them, but she put the books in the tote bag Mrs. Harris had given her so they would be safe.

Sharon's father and even her mother were impressed with the gift. Her mother apologized to Sharon for not having gotten herself together to do anything about Christmas.

Three days later, Mrs. Harris was back. Snickers was standoffish with her at first, punishing her for having gone away as Mrs. Harris put it, but Sharon was unabashedly glad to see her. And she was right. Mrs. Harris had relented on the question of the Narnia books, and they were going to try the first one, *The Lion, the Witch and the Wardrobe* as soon as they read one more book, *Nancy and Plum*, which was a story partly about Christmas, written by Betty MacDonald, author of the better-known Mrs. Piggle-Wiggle books.

Nancy and Plum (Pamela really) were two little girls, orphans, whose bachelor uncle had boarded them at a terrible place. Their adventures as they tried to make their lives more tolerable had made the book a favorite with Mrs. Harris when she was ten years old. Sharon found that she loved it, too, and the illustrations were good.

They had lots of time to read and moved through the book quickly. Mrs. Stover had to go back to work the day after New Year's Day, so Sharon was spending three whole days with Mrs. Harris before the weekend. School would start again on the following Monday. Mrs. Harris didn't mind watching Sharon, and they found lots to do. Sharon re-read all of Mrs. Harris's picture books, and they went for a walk every day. One day, they even made a trip back to the downtown library.

Fr. Karimu came to tea on the following Thursday. He reported that he hadn't yet heard back from the bishop about his request to baptize Sharon in her father's hospital room, but that he wasn't surprised as Christmas was such a busy season for bishops and priests. He planned to see if he could get an answer the next day, now that the New Year's holiday was over.

Sharon and Mrs. Harris showed him how Sharon had learned all three prayers from the list that he had left with them. She was also able to give at least a simple answer to his questions about the love of God, sin, and how the Eucharist was different from bread.

"Okay," he agreed at the end of the session. "You are ready, and I am willing to baptize you if the bishop will give his permission."

"We've been wondering something," Mrs. Harris said. "Has Sharon's father had any ideas about godparents?"

"We talked about it," answered Fr. Karimu. "You will be her godmother, won't you?"

"Yes, of course, that's what we thought," answered Mrs. Harris, smiling at Sharon, who smiled back. "But what about a godfather?"

"There do not seem to be any relatives who could do it," answered Fr. Karimu.

"Could you be my godfather?" Sharon asked in a hesitating voice, not knowing if priests ever were godfathers. Even Mrs. Harris hadn't known the answer to that one.

"I could, but then we would need a different priest to baptize you," answered Fr. Karimu. "I can do either one or the other, but not both."

"Oh," said Sharon.

"But I think you would rather that I baptize you. In either case, I *am* your spiritual father, and I am not going to lose track of you. And you are being educated in the faith now, which is the job of godparents if parents cannot do it, so I do not think you really need more than Mama Wilma. She is a host in herself," he said, giving Mrs. Harris a look.

Sharon nodded. "I guess that's okay," she said. "I wouldn't want you not to baptize me."

Fr. Karimu called the next day while Sharon was there. Mrs. Harris took the call. Partway through it, she put her hand over the receiver and said to Sharon, "The bishop said yes. Fr. Karimu is calling from your father's room at the hospital. They're thinking that tomorrow will be a good day to baptize you. What do you think?"

"Oh my gosh, tomorrow?" asked Sharon.

"Yes, Saturday. That way your mom can be there, too."

"Well, yeah. Yeah, I guess so. Oh my gosh," repeated Sharon.

"Two o'clock," said Mrs. Harris. She reported to Fr. Karimu that Sharon agreed to the plan, then ended the phone call.

Chapter 16

The Baptism

A small group assembled in Sharon's father's hospital room just before two o'clock the next day. Sharon and her mother got there first, but Fr. Karimu arrived soon after, followed shortly by Mrs. Harris. Fr. Karimu had to organize a small table and a bowl to hold water for the baptism. The VA nurses were helpful and seemed intrigued. This wasn't an everyday occurrence. Several of them stood in the hallway just outside the door and watched the proceedings.

Fr. Karimu put water in the bowl, made a quick sign of the cross over the water as he asked God to bless it, and laid a couple of small towels next to the bowl on the table. Then he put a bottle of holy oil and a candle next to the towels. He didn't light the candle but just left it lying on the table.

He had taken off his coat when he walked into the room. Now he put a stole, a strip of cloth, around his neck, white-colored for the Christmas season. He handed everyone a few sheets of paper with the rite of baptism printed on them, then started right in.

Sharon answered "yes" to the question of whether she wanted to be baptized, then renounced the devil "and all his works," as the ceremony went on.

Sharon's father and Mrs. Harris promised to do all in their power to support Sharon in her walk with Christ. Fr. Karimu baptized Sharon "in the Name of the Father, and of the Son, and of the Holy Spirit," dipping his cupped hand into the water three times and letting the water run over her head and forehead. Then, he blotted up the dripping water with one of the towels and anointed her with holy oil from the bottle, marking her as Christ's own forever.

Now, he lit the candle and handed it to Mrs. Harris, who handed it to Sharon. He explained that the candle represented moving from death to life in Christ. After a minute or two, Sharon blew out the candle, having asked if that was all right. She got to keep it though.

Everyone exchanged hugs, and the baptism was over.

Sharon's dad remarked, "Well, that's one thing off my conscience. Thank you, Father," to Fr. Karimu.

On Sunday, Sharon went to Mass with Mrs. Harris, the 8:30 AM Mass this time. Epiphany was celebrated, a day early, and Sharon got to hear "We Three Kings" for the first time outside of the school yard. Previously, she had only known it as a song where a king tried to smoke a rubber cigar, so she was surprised to learn that it was a real hymn and a lovely one at that.

The next day, Mrs. Harris and Snickers met Sharon outside her school for the first time in two weeks. "Today, it's really Epiphany," Mrs. Harris commented. "The Wise Men need to arrive when we get back to my house, and I made some spice cookies and frosted them so we could celebrate."

"Oh, neat!" Sharon smiled. "You know your spice cookies are my favorite thing, right?"

Mrs. Harris nodded. "I like them, too," she agreed, "especially with frosting."

"And the Wise Men are finally arriving. Wow! Then do you put the whole thing away?" Sharon was worried.

"Not yet a while. They can stay out until just before Lent. That's the length of the old season of Epiphany."

"Let's hurry," begged Sharon.

A few days later, they finished *Nancy and Plum* and were ready to start the Narnia books. "I think that *The Lion, the Witch and the Wardrobe* is the right book to start with on the first time through them," said Mrs. Harris. "When you read them yourself, later on, you might want to use chronological order."

"What's that?" asked Sharon.

"Chronological order means time order. Reading the book that happened in the earliest year, then the one that happened in the next earliest year, and so on. That would mean *The Magician's Nephew* would come first—but for the first reading I think it's better to keep to the order in which C. S. Lewis wrote the books."

"Oh," Sharon nodded.

It was hard going at first. Mrs. Harris didn't paraphrase, but she did have to explain certain words and old-fashioned Britishisms. After a while, however, the story swept Sharon into it, and she forgot about the difficulties. They made good progress through *The Lion, the Witch and the Wardrobe*. Sharon was intrigued by Prof. Kirk's big, old house, never having seen or imagined such a place. And she loved the idea of a closet full of real fur coats. She had had a fake fur coat when she was about four years old, the sort of coat that most grown-ups find inappropriate, but which appeals to little girls of a certain age and in which they are sometimes indulged.

Sharon's coat had been pure white. It had come with a matching muff on a string and the muff had a red and blue appliquéd Scottie dog on it. She had thought then that it was the most beautiful coat in the world, in its soft whiteness. She still did. The day her mom had pronounced it outgrown still gave Sharon a twinge of regret when she thought of it. So, she liked the idea of a wardrobe full of soft fur.

Likewise, the faun and the talking beavers delighted her. Her favorite picture so far was the one of Mrs. Beaver sitting at her sewing machine.

The White Witch scared her, though, and she had to ask several anxious questions about whether or not everything was going to come out all right before they could continue.

When Aslan appeared, Sharon loved him at once. Mrs. Harris explained that he was supposed to be like Jesus, then, laughing, added that she had read the books for five years before finding that out.

"I loved Aslan, too," she said. It was snack time, and they were sitting in the kitchen, Mrs. Harris with her usual cup of tea, Sharon with half a sandwich and a glass of cold milk, and Snickers with his dog biscuit.

"I was ten when I discovered the Narnia books, but I had no idea in the world that they had anything to do with Jesus. Then, when I was fifteen, I read that Aslan was meant to be Jesus, and it really surprised me. Do you know why C. S. Lewis wrote the Narnia books?" she asked.

Sharon shook her head, her mouth too full to answer.

"Well, do you remember telling me about how you went to Sunday School with a friend and didn't like it?"

"Did I tell you about that?"

Mrs. Harris nodded in turn. "Well, I read a letter C. S. Lewis wrote to somebody saying that he wrote the Narnia books to give children an idea of what Jesus is really like and to counteract the atmosphere of old maid Sunday School teachers and cold linoleum."

Sharon laughed. "What's an old maid, and what's linoleum?"

"An old maid is a woman who never married, and linoleum is an old kind of hard floor, not carpet and not wood, sort of like the vinyl floors of today."

"Oh, well then, are a lot of Sunday Schools that way? I remember the cold, hard floor."

"I think so," admitted Mrs. Harris. "I ran into a couple of them myself when I was a child. Anyway, I loved Aslan with all my heart, and I tried so hard to believe in him. Once or twice, I almost succeeded, but the problem was that in the back of my mind I knew the books were fiction... Let's go read."

When Aslan was killed, Sharon couldn't believe it was really going to happen. She found herself with tears pouring down her cheeks when she finally had to believe that he was dead.

Mrs. Harris squeezed her shoulder and said she had felt the same way the first time she read the book.

"But he didn't do anything wrong," wailed Sharon. "It's so unfair!"

"Yes, it is," agreed Mrs. Harris.

"And the White Witch wins!"

"She seems to win, but remember there's more of the story."

Finally, Sharon managed to stop crying. But all evening, whenever she thought of Aslan being dead tears came to her eyes again. And that night she cried herself to sleep.

The next day, when Aslan came to life again, Sharon was astounded. Could that really happen, she wanted to know. Could someone really come back to life after being dead?

Mrs. Harris reminded her that it had happened with Jesus and that then He never had to die again.

"But why didn't you tell me?" Sharon asked, looking at Mrs. Harris reproachfully.

"Well, what if I had told you?" asked Mrs. Harris in turn. "Do you think you would be as happy as you are now?"

"Maybe not," conceded Sharon.

"Usually, if you want joy you have to have pain, too. Myself, I think it's worth it. What do you think?"

"I don't know," Sharon said slowly.

Mrs. Harris continued, "Think about this. You may read these books many times in the years to come, but you'll never cry over Aslan's death the way you did yesterday. It's a gift, really. The first time I read *The Lion, the Witch and the Wardrobe*," she continued, "I just had to put the book down and cry for a long time. I couldn't believe Aslan was really dead."

"I know," said Sharon. "I felt the same way because that usually never happens in books for children."

"Yes, that's true," agreed Mrs. Harris.

That day, Sharon noticed that the pictures on the living room wall had been changed a bit. A couple of small ones were gone, and there was a big framed poster where they had been. When she went to look at it, she realized that it was a map of Narnia.

"Oh, how wonderful," she breathed and, fetching a chair, stood on it, studying everything about the map.

Mrs. Harris pointed out some things to her, the places that they had read about so far: Lantern Waste, the castle of the White Witch, Mr. and Mrs. Beaver's house.

"Where did you get it?" Sharon asked.

"This map? You know, I've had it so many years that I really don't remember. The good thing is that I had it framed. That's why it stayed safe, even while I was in Africa, and it was in storage. It usually hangs in my study, but you hardly ever go there so I thought I'd move it out here."

Chapter 17

God?

About a week after this, Mrs. Harris noticed that Sharon was acting rather oddly as they walked home from school. She glanced sideways at Mrs. Harris, took a deep breath as though to speak, then said
nothing as she apparently changed her mind. They walked on a little
way, then Mrs. Harris saw the same thing happen again: the sideways glance, a deep breath, followed by silence. After the third time,
she looked down at Sharon, chuckled, and invited her to "spit it out."

Sharon smiled, but she also blushed.

"It's a secret," she said.

"Well, there's nobody around," rejoined Mrs. Harris.

But just then a little boy on a red tricycle turned the corner up
ahead of them and started down the sidewalk toward them, followed
by his mother, who had a large black dog on a leash.

Mrs. Harris bent down and gathered Snickers up in her arms. He
was always foolhardy when they crossed paths with another dog. He
could not be kept from barking his head off and seemed willing to
fight even the largest dog.

There were several seconds of barking dogs. The other woman
had to hold her dog's leash hard and pull with all her strength to
keep her dog from taking up Snickers's ill-considered challenge. The
two women smiled apologetically at each other as they met. Then
things calmed down, and Mrs. Harris and Sharon finished the walk
home.

"So, did you want to tell me something?" asked Mrs. Harris, once they were settled at the kitchen table.

Sharon blushed again. "Yes, but it's kind of … I don't know what you'll think," she said. "You're the only one I could tell, besides maybe Daddy or Mama, but…"

"Don't if you don't want to," suggested Mrs. Harris.

"No, it's … well, it's just that I believe in God now," blurted out Sharon.

"You do?" Mrs. Harris smiled broadly. "Well, that's good news. How did that happen?"

"It was last night," said Sharon. "I woke up in the middle of the night, 'cause I heard a noise. I was really, really scared," she admitted, looking up at Mrs. Harris, who nodded sympathetically.

"I couldn't even move, I was so scared—see, I wanted to run and get in bed with Mama, but I couldn't. I couldn't even move," she repeated. "Does that happen with other children?" she asked, troubled. "Did it ever happen to you when you were little?"

Mrs. Harris nodded slowly, remembering. "Yes, yes it did," she replied. "Not often, but I can think of twice anyway when it happened."

"Well, I thought of what you said about praying, and I just said, 'Help!' inside myself. You know…" She looked at Mrs. Harris to see if she did know.

Mrs. Harris nodded again and made that sound that means yes.

"Like, I was talking to God and asking Him for help. And He helped me—He really did," she said earnestly. "It was like He reached down and held my hand."

She looked up at Mrs. Harris again to make sure she was still following the story.

"I mean, not really, you know—like I didn't *see* a hand—but He really was there, and I felt so comforted. And I just lay there like that, like we were holding hands, until I fell asleep again."

"What a beautiful story," commented Mrs. Harris. "Isn't God good?"

"So, now I really, really believe in God," finished Sharon, "'cause before I wasn't quite sure..."

"But why is it a secret?" Mrs. Harris asked, getting up to clear the table.

"Oh," Sharon blushed for the third time. "It just seems kind of private, you know. And I don't think my Mama would like it."

"Don't you?" wondered Mrs. Harris. "Be careful about that. In one of the Gospels, Jesus says that if you acknowledge Him before men, He will acknowledge you to His Father, but if you deny Him, He'll deny you."

"Oh, gosh," said Sharon.

"Just something to keep in mind," said Mrs. Harris. "You're a beginner, and you can't learn everything all in an instant. Anyway, it's wonderful news," she continued. "And look at the timing. You were just baptized a few weeks ago."

"Yeah, I noticed that, too," said Sharon. "Do you know, I don't think I'm going to be so afraid any more. Because if God's really there and can comfort me, then I don't need to be afraid, do I?"

Mrs. Harris agreed and pointed out that in her opinion Sharon had been gradually losing her fears and had made considerable progress already. "I mean, just look how you were with that big black dog just now. You didn't panic, did you? You just walked close to me."

"Maybe it's because I love Snickers so much now," suggested Sharon. "It makes other dogs look less scary."

"Yes, maybe," responded Mrs. Harris. "You know, I don't think you have any really irrational fears."

"What does that mean?" asked Sharon, through a mouthful of peanut butter sandwich.

"It means you're scared of real things. The problem is that you've been *too* scared," answered Mrs. Harris. "Bad things do happen, but they don't happen very often to any particular person.

"And now that you believe in God, you'll see. Because if things get bad, God seems to draw closer, even though really He's probably that close all along. Still, it *seems* that way. Like last night you were scared, which is bad of course… but God comforted you, which is very good. I think it's better to be comforted by God than it is bad to be scared, if you see what I mean."

Sharon nodded and thought that over. "Is it always that way?"

"Yes, I think it is," said Mrs. Harris. The times I've been in the most pain have also been the times I've felt closest to God when I look back on them later. It's very noticeable."

They went to read then, but Sharon thought back to that conversation later.

As they were walking home from school one day toward the beginning of February, Sharon seemed happier than usual. She kept breaking into skipping, even in her snow boots. Several times, Mrs. Harris caught her smiling happily to herself.

Mrs. Harris was carrying Snickers, who had gotten ice stuck between his toes on the way to fetch Sharon and wasn't willing to be put down.

"Would you like me to carry Snickers?" Sharon offered. "I'd love to."

"Well, sure," agreed Mrs. Harris. "It's no great pleasure for me to carry him."

She handed Snickers over. "Although I don't suppose I'd want to walk barefooted—bare-pawed?—out here. You seem happy today," she added.

"I've got something to show you," Sharon sparkled. "At snack. A surprise."

Mrs. Harris nodded. "I can't wait."

Once they were settled at the kitchen table, Snickers having had his paws de-iced and dried, Sharon opened up her backpack and began to dig. She came up with a folder and the *First Communion Catechism* that Fr. Karimu had given her. Fr. Karimu and Sharon, with frequent comments by Mrs. Harris, had gone through a lesson on each of the two previous Thursdays when he had come to tea. Each time, Sharon had written the answers to the questions at the end of the chapters as homework then showed them to Mrs. Harris.

Now, she gave Mrs. Harris the folder she had dug out of her backpack.

"Look," she said, "I thought I'd work ahead." Words poured out of her, "'Cause now that I believe in God I really, really want to make my first Communion. I'm already two years behind. I've got extra time at school, so I thought I'd just see how much I could do by myself. See, 'cause we get time to study at school, and I usually don't need it all, so I used to read or maybe draw pictures, but I've been studying this book and writing out the answers to the questions at the ends of the chapters." She paused for a much-needed breath after this torrent of words.

Mrs. Harris was turning over page after page in the folder.

"You've done a lot of work," she commented.

"Yeah, I finished chapter nine today, and there are only two more. And I've been memorizing the other prayers and stuff. I haven't done absolutely everything, but I've done most of it."

"I'm really impressed," said Mrs. Harris.

Sharon smiled but started to squirm in her seat, "I kind of hoped Fr. Karimu might let me in early," she said. "'Cause May seems so far away. So, I just thought…" Her voice trailed off.

"Hmm…," mused Mrs. Harris. "He's coming to tea on Thursday as usual. That's just a few days away. Let's talk to him then. Would you like me to look this over," she gestured at the folder, "and correct anything that needs correcting?"

Sharon nodded eagerly. "And we could talk about it. And maybe you could hear what I've memorized?"

"Sure," agreed Mrs. Harris. "Give me till tomorrow. I'll have looked it all over by then. And you go ahead and finish the last two chapters."

On Thursday they waited until Fr. Karimu was settled at the kitchen table and had helped himself to tea. Mrs. Harris was cutting up two juicy-looking mangoes.

"Sharon has a surprise for you," she said, as she worked with one of the mangoes.

Fr. Karimu looked at Sharon, who blushed.

Mrs. Harris went on. "She's been working ahead in the cate-chism book you gave her and has just about finished it. Show him your folder, Sharon."

Sharon gave him the folder, which had been lying next to her plate at the table.

"Mrs. Harris has corrected all but the last two chapters," she said.

Fr. Karimu looked over the thick wad of papers with a smile on his face.

"I've gone over her answers, and she's done a lot of good work," confirmed Mrs. Harris, handing around plates of mango. "We've talked about the questions," she assured him, "and there were a few things to clear up but not many. She has also learned many of the prayers."

"Which ones?" asked Fr. Karimu, serious now.

Sharon pulled the *First Communion Catechism* out of her back-pack and opened it.

"All the ones before Chapter 1," she said. "Well, most of those I'd already learned to be baptized. But I learned the rest. And at the back," she continued, "the Apostles' Creed and the seven sacraments and the ten commandments, but I forget some of those sometimes, but that's what I'm working on now."

"Could you recite for me the Apostles' Creed?" Fr. Karimu asked.

Sharon gulped, took a deep breath and started in, "I believe in God, the Father Almighty…" She got through it without any trouble, and Fr. Karimu nodded.

"Very nice."

"But I've just got one question, though," said Sharon. "What's 'thence,' like 'from thence He shall come to judge the living and the dead'?"

Fr. Karimu looked at Mrs. Harris. "English teacher?" he asked.

Mrs. Harris smiled. "'Thence' is a word from an older English than we use these days," she explained. "We usually just say 'there' now. In fact, more modern versions of the Apostles' Creed say, 'from there He shall come.' But the way it used to be was that 'thence' told you a direction of motion—that something was coming from farther away toward the hearer. The opposite of that, from near to farther away, was 'thither.' So, there were three: if it was not moving it was 'there.' If it was coming toward you it was 'thence.' And if it was moving away from you it was 'thither.' And to change them to question words it would be 'where,' 'whence' and 'whither,'" she finished.

Fr. Karimu looked at Sharon. "I did not know any of that," he said. "I am glad you asked."

"So why did we stop doing it?" Sharon asked. "It's kind of cool."

"There isn't any 'why' to it, I don't think," answered Mrs. Harris. "Languages change and evolve. It's just a fact. These days we use prepositions to do the same job: 'from where,' 'to where,' and so on."

"I kind of like 'thence' and 'whence,'" said Sharon.

"You'll find them in literature," said Mrs. Harris. "Later on, when you study Shakespeare for example. Even in nursery rhymes maybe. I bet you could find some in that big Mother Goose book of mine."

"I'm going to go see," said Sharon, jumping up.

"Yes, but wait a sec," Mrs. Harris gestured her to sit down.

"So, the point of all this," Mrs. Harris said to Fr. Karimu, "is that Sharon was hoping you could think of a way for her to make her first Communion sooner than May, since she's already a fourth grader. It was her own idea. That's why she did all that work."

Fr. Karimu nodded while he thought about that. "You have certainly worked hard," he said to Sharon, "and if Mama Wilma says that your work is good…"

Mrs. Harris nodded.

"So, I think you know enough. Of course, you would have to make your first Confession, too. I have an idea," he continued. "In a few weeks, a family is going to make a profession of faith at Mass and come into the Church. They are a man, his wife, and their children, all of them receiving whatever sacraments they need. It seems to me that the mother needs only to be confirmed, but the father and the children need more. They have been working with the Rector of the Cathedral, the other priest," he explained to Sharon. "Sometimes, people are not made to go through all the classes for various reasons. Let me talk with the Rector and with your father. Perhaps you could make your first Communion then if everyone agrees. It is happening before Lent, so that's good because otherwise we would probably have to wait until after Easter."

Sharon looked at him, a big smile on her face. "Just a few weeks maybe?" she asked. "Not that long?"

"Maybe," he answered. "I will see what I can do and let you know as soon as I can."

After a long weekend of waiting, Mrs. Harris told Sharon, when she picked her up from school the next Monday, that the change of

plan had been approved by everyone. She herself would take Sharon
to make her first Confession, a week from Saturday, then the next
day at the 8:30 AM Sunday Mass Sharon and the other family would
be received into the Church, make first Communions, be confirmed
or baptized, whatever needed to be done. Apparently, there were a
couple of small children who would need to be baptized. Since the
Rector had been working with the family, he would be the main cel-
ebrant at that Mass, but Fr. Karimu said he would concelebrate, even
though he had to do the 11 o'clock Mass as well.

The next time Sharon went to visit her father, she found that he
was happy to have things moving so quickly and was happier yet that
Sharon had worked so hard. He had been out of the hospital again,
but was now back in. Sharon had grown accustomed to life either
way. She worried less about him in the hospital. He wouldn't have
been able to come to her first Communion even if he had been at
home, but of course she was sorry he couldn't come. So was he.

Chapter 18

First Communion

Sharon's first confession, when Mrs. Harris took her, went well. Sharon was nervous, of course, but it helped a lot to have Mrs. Harris there, standing behind her in line. They had talked about the "how-tos" of confession in the car on the way there. Sharon had her *First Communion Catechism* along, marked at the right page for confession. The book laid out everything that she needed to do. She was worried that she would forget the act of contrition. She had memorized it, but it was in a different part of the book, so if she needed to refer to it, she would have to turn the pages to find it.

Nothing went wrong, though. The priest wasn't Fr. Karimu, but he was kind and helped Sharon get through the confession when she told him that it was her first one. An act of contrition was on a printed card sitting on the kneeler, right there in front of her, where she couldn't miss seeing it.

Sharon came out feeling as though she was walking on air, almost giddy with relief, then knelt down in a pew to say the three "Hail Marys" that were her penance while she waited for Mrs. Harris to finish her confession.

The next day, Sunday, Sharon was up early. She had taken a bath the night before without being reminded to and had thought a lot about what to wear for first Communion in the days that preceded it. She had actually prevailed on her mother to buy her a new dress.

It was a white knitted dress with embroidered flowers in various pastel colors. With it she wore tights and her best shoes, the half boots of brown leather. Her mother tied back her hair with a pink ribbon which matched some of the dress's flowers. She looked nice, and Mrs. Harris complimented her when she and her mother went over to Mrs. Harris's house to get a ride to the Cathedral.

Mrs. Stover rode up front with Mrs. Harris, and they chatted all the way there. Sharon sat in back, listening to the grown-ups talk and looking out the car window.

"It's such a pity my husband can't come," remarked Sharon's mother. "He's very sorry to miss it."

"Let's take some pictures after Mass," offered Mrs. Harris. "I brought a disposable camera along just in case."

"Oh, Jim will be so pleased," said Sharon's mother. "There's a one-hour photo place open on Sunday, isn't there? I could drop the film off, then take Sharon home for lunch, and we could pick up the pictures on the way to the VA Hospital this afternoon."

"That's a good idea," agreed Mrs. Harris.

Sharon watched the city slide by as they headed downtown to the Cathedral. Colors looked brighter to her than usual, perhaps because it was a gray day. The traffic lights were particularly vivid, their greens, yellows, and reds shining like jewels.

She was keyed up about what was going to happen, but, after all, it wasn't much of an ordeal. Sharon, her mother, and Mrs. Harris sat together in the second pew, which was marked "Reserved." The other family sat in the first pew. That family had to go up for the baptisms of the children. The man made a profession of faith, then both of the adults were confirmed by the Rector of the Cathedral.

Sharon watched but didn't understand everything that happened. The baptism part was familiar, though, and candles were given to both of the children.

Receiving Communion was much easier. An announcement was made about the family and Sharon making their first Communions, and Sharon went forward right after the family in the first pew—just in front of Mrs. Harris. Her mother stayed seated and didn't come forward at all.

For the first time, Sharon didn't have to cross her arms to ask for a blessing. She had practiced receiving the Eucharist with Mrs. Harris (they had used rice crackers!), so she did that part okay and soon found herself back in the pew, kneeling beside Mrs. Harris.

After Mass, there was a small reception downstairs for the family and for Sharon. Sharon was surprised to see that it seemed to be a present-giving occasion. She was even more surprised to receive presents herself. Fr. Karimu gave her a crucifix about 6 inches tall, which he said she could hang up in her room. The family of converts received one as well, Sharon realized, as she saw the parents with the same kind of box that her crucifix came in.

They all received rosaries and cards about how to pray the Rosary. These came from a women's group at the Cathedral. Her rosary was beautiful, Sharon thought. The beads on it looked like pink pearls, and the chains between beads, as well as the crucifix, were silver colored. She was delighted with it.

But the gift of gifts was the one Mrs. Harris gave her. She apologized for it not being a conventional first Communion gift, as well as being out of season, but said she thought it might be what Sharon would like best. And, indeed, it was. It was a nativity set like Mrs.

Harris's own. Mrs. Harris said she had noticed how much Sharon enjoyed playing with hers at Christmas, so here was one she could play whenever she wanted to.

"Can I keep it out even though it's not Christmastime?" Sharon asked.

"I don't see any harm in that," replied Mrs. Harris. "After all, it's yours."

Mrs. Harris had given her a "starter set," the basic figures of St. Mary, St. Joseph, the baby Jesus, an angel for the roof, a manger, and a stable. But she pointed out to Sharon that from now on people would have a pretty good idea of what to give her for Christmas, probably starting with a king and maybe a camel. And the stable was special, just like Mrs. Harris's one. The roof had a little bit of moss on it and tiny little pine cones.

Mrs. Harris also took the pictures she had discussed with Mrs. Stover, partly for herself as she said, but mostly for Sharon's father. There was a picture of Sharon with Fr. Karimu; one with Sharon, Fr. Karimu, and Mrs. Harris; several of Sharon alone; and one with her mother; then a picture of all four of them. Another parishioner helped out by taking the pictures that involved Mrs. Harris. They finished the roll and Sharon's mother took it, promising to get double prints made.

Neither Sharon nor her mother felt much like eating lunch, having had cake, cookies, and hors d'œuvres at the reception, so after Mrs. Harris drove them home, they got into their own car and took the film to the one-hour developer, then walked around the store and the mall it was in while they waited for the pictures to be ready.

They headed for the VA Hospital as soon as they had the pictures in hand.

Sharon's mother didn't say much about the Mass or Sharon's first Communion in the car, but she did comment on how nice everyone seemed.

"Mama, were you ever baptized?" Sharon asked.

"Oh, sure, when I was a baby," replied her mother. "Everybody was in those days. But I never went to church much. My parents made me go to Sunday school when I was little, but I quit as soon as I was too old for them to make me go anymore."

"Why? Didn't you like it?" asked her daughter.

"Oh, I don't know," Mrs. Stover replied. "I guess it just didn't seem very relevant to my life… Maybe it wasn't a very good Sunday school," she added after reflecting silently for a moment. "They didn't seem to teach us much. We just played around, then had juice and graham crackers is all I remember."

"'Cause I don't know too much about it yet, but I do believe in God now," said Sharon. "It seems so important to me. Finding out what happens when you die. I want to know more about God."

"Yeah, I suppose so," admitted her mother. "I don't think anybody really knows, though."

"But, Mama, what if they do? What if there really is a God and He really did make a reason for us to be alive?"

"Then, I guess He forgot to tell me about it," her mother joked.

They were almost at the VA hospital. Sharon looked up at the big sign and suddenly thought of a different question.

"Mama, what is a VA, anyway?" she asked.

"Veteran's Administration, Hon. Didn't you know that?" Her mother seemed surprised.

"But what's a veteran?"

"A veteran is anyone who's been in the armed forces—you know, Army, Navy, Marines, whatever," her mother replied as she parked the car in the big parking lot. It was always crowded on the weekend, so they had quite a ways to walk to get to the building.

"Was Daddy in one of those?" Sharon asked.

"You knew he was in the Army, didn't you?"

"I don't think so," Sharon said doubtfully.

"Yeah, well he was. He really hated it, so he doesn't talk much about it," her mother explained. "But that was before you were born. Before we were married even. It's good, though, because now when he's sick he can get treated here. If it weren't for that I don't know what we'd do," she sighed. "If there were huge medical bills on top of everything else…" her voice trailed off.

The pictures had come out well, and Sharon's father was very pleased to see them. He sighed, though, and said he wished he could have been there. "All those years I could have gone to church, and I didn't," he said regretfully. "Now I'd give anything to go, but I can't."

The chaplain for the hospital brought him Holy Communion every other day or so, or Fr. Karimu did when he visited, either at home or in the hospital, and for that he was grateful, but it wasn't the same as going to church.

He encouraged Sharon to keep going and wrung a reluctant promise from her mother not to interfere with that, ever. Sharon had told him about Christmas and having to call Fr. Karimu to get to

Mass. She remembered the promise later and wondered if he knew then that he wouldn't be around to make sure she went.

Sharon had insisted on bringing her presents in to show her dad. He liked them, too, and asked if he could borrow the rosary. Sharon didn't know how to use it yet and anyway was glad to leave it with him now. It was one of their better visits, what with all the news to share and pictures and presents to show.

Chapter 19

Lots of Talk

Lent started as February ended. Everything at church was purple—vestments, altar cloth, pulpit, and lectern scarves. Mrs. Harris pointed out to Sharon that purple was the color both for Advent and for Lent.

As March wore on, Sharon noticed that her father hadn't been out of the hospital for quite a while. Fr. Karimu usually visited him once a week, as he had been doing for several months, whether Sharon's father was at home or in the hospital. He prayed with him and brought him Communion.

Sharon didn't know what they talked about, but she noticed that her father seemed more and more peaceful. He was in pain quite often. He took pain medication, but only when the pain was so bad that he felt he "had to," as it tended to put him to sleep. He didn't like "sleeping his life away," as he put it.

During one of Fr. Karimu's visits for tea and talk, Sharon found the courage to ask him if he thought her father was dying. Her parents hadn't ever talked to her about it since that one frank talk and when she asked her mother, the answer was always "of course not," but Sharon had her doubts about it. She hadn't heard any more talk about him being in remission, and it seemed to her that her dad was weaker all the time and looked sicker and sicker. When he was at home, she got used to the way he looked and didn't see the gradual worsening of his condition, but it was harder to miss when he was in the hospital and she only saw him on the weekends.

So, failing to get a straight answer from her mother and being unwilling to broach the topic with her dad, she asked Fr. Karimu one Thursday.

"Do you think my daddy is going to die?"

He gave her a quiet, serious look and replied, "Yes, I think he probably is. He isn't getting any better, is he? In fact, he seems to keep going downhill bit by bit."

This was what Sharon had feared, but it still brought tears to her eyes.

"Why?" she whispered through her tears. Blinking hard, she looked up at Fr. Karimu's face again and saw that he, too, had tears in his eyes.

"It is one of the hardest things," he answered. "Remember what I told you when we first met? Death is such a powerful enemy that God, Himself, had to die to conquer it."

"But then if God conquered it, why does my daddy still have to die?" asked Sharon.

"When we say that God conquered death, it means that your father will be with God after he dies. The gates of heaven are open because Jesus died and rose from the dead. God will take good care of your father."

"But I want him here," sobbed Sharon. "I don't want him to die."

"I know," said the priest. "And he does not want to leave you either. It is always hardest for mothers or fathers of young children if they have to die. But he does not get to choose."

By now he had reached across the table and was holding her hand. Tears were running down her cheeks. He pulled out a clean handkerchief and gently wiped her face.

Sharon gulped and tried to smile.

"Thank you for telling me. The hardest part is not knowing what's going on. I needed to know."

They stood up from the kitchen table. Fr. Karimu walked around it and gave her a hug,

"Well, I have to go," he said. "May I tell your father that you know about this when I visit him tomorrow?"

Sharon thought for a few seconds, then sighed. "I guess so," she said at last. "If you think you should."

"Thank you," replied Fr. Karimu. Mrs. Harris walked him to the front door. When she came back, Sharon was still standing in the same place. She sighed again, and shook herself, then went to the front closet for her coat. It was time to go home. Her mother had quit calling every day by now, but just counted on Sharon and Mrs. Harris to notice her car in the driveway once she was home.

"Do you want to talk about it?" asked Mrs. Harris.

Sharon shook her head. "Not today. Tomorrow maybe?"

They had finished their first run through the Narnia books. Sharon was re-reading them on her own, in chronological order this time. She and Mrs. Harris were now in the middle of a book called *When Hitler Stole Pink Rabbit*, and Sharon was interested in this story of a girl whose family flees Hitler's Germany and who has to learn French. She particularly liked it when Mrs. Harris showed her what some of the phrases sounded like in that language.

A couple of days later, though, *When Hitler Stole Pink Rabbit* led to a further discussion about bad things happening in the world. Sharon hadn't studied about World War II in school yet, and was surprised and appalled to hear about the tens of millions of people who had died in that war, and the many millions who had died in the preceding World War I. After Mrs. Harris explained a little about the scope of the two wars, Sharon couldn't help wondering out loud how it could be that such bad things could happen.

Mrs. Harris took a deep breath, looked gravely at Sharon, and said, "Now you're asking one of the important questions, one of the questions that people have been asking for as long as the world has existed. I can give you part of an answer, Sharon, but you need to understand that this is really a grown-up question, and you're going to have to grow into the answer."

"What do you mean?" asked Sharon.

"Well, I mean that although nobody understands the whole thing, you can't expect, at the age of nine, to understand even as much as a grown-up who has been thinking about it off and on for years would. The more you learn about it, the more you'll understand, but don't expect to understand it all right away today, okay?"

Sharon nodded, but her eyes were shining. She had an endearing way of speaking frankly, sometimes, and she did it now.

"You know what one of the things I like the best about you is?" she asked.

"No, what?" asked Mrs. Harris in return, smiling.

"I like the way you talk to me like I'm a real person. I mean, you don't ever talk down to me or treat me like a baby. You know how some grown-ups, like they'll use this funny kind of voice when they talk to children?"

Mrs. Harris was nodding. Now she put on a high-pitched tone of voice and said, "And how are *we* today? Have we been a good girl?"

Sharon laughed until she almost choked. "That's it!" she said when she could speak again.

"And they kneel down and talk right into your face, right?" pursued Mrs. Harris.

Sharon nodded, still laughing. "Sometimes."

"Yeah, well I hated both those things, too, when I was a child," said Mrs. Harris.

"Oh…" Sharon looked thoughtful. "Oh, that's why… So, you remember being a child?"

"Oh, yes," Mrs. Harris was very definite. "I remember my childhood better than my adult life."

"Does everyone?" Sharon asked.

"No, I don't think so. I've often met adults who say they don't remember much at all about being a child. But lots of us do. That's why it's so unfair when grown-ups fight with children, by the way. We remember all the tricks we used when we were your age."

They abandoned the reading by unspoken consent and moved over to the fireplace, where a fire was laid, ready to light. Mrs. Harris lit it, and they both sat down on the big sheepskin rug that lay in front of the fireplace. After a minute, Sharon stretched out on her side, choosing a place where she could watch Mrs. Harris and the fire without having to move her head much. One of the odd things about Mrs. Harris, from Sharon's point of view, was that unlike the other grown-ups that Sharon knew, she liked sitting on the floor and quite often did. Either she sat cross-legged or, as now, sat hugging her knees loosely, at least as much as a stout person could. They both stared into the fire as it gained strength, the flames licking the edges of the rolled-up newspapers and starting the smaller sticks of kindling on fire.

"I just love fires," remarked Mrs. Harris.

Sharon agreed. She loved them, too.

"They're a lot of work," continued Mrs. Harris. "You have to sweep out the fireplace and put the ashes into a metal bucket for a few days to make sure they're really out, but I think it's worth it."

"Why don't you have gas logs?" asked Sharon. "We used to have gas logs in our other house."

"Because I like real things," replied Mrs. Harris shortly. "But you were asking about evil in the world."

"Right," said Sharon.

"Well, for a start," said Mrs. Harris, "Jesus talked about it. He said, 'Don't be afraid. In this world, you'll have trouble, but I have overcome the world.'"

"But couldn't God stop the evil?" asked Sharon.

"He could, of course, agreed Mrs. Harris. "The thing seems to be, though, that He thinks free will is important. I don't suppose you know what free will is."

"No," agreed Sharon. "What?"

"Well, it means that we can really choose. Like in the garden of Eden when Adam and Eve chose to eat the apple even though God had told them not to. So, it means that we really, truly are free to choose. And ever since Adam and Eve, people have sometimes been choosing to do bad things. Not everybody all the time, but all of us, sometimes. That's what Jesus came to save us from."

"But why would God want us to have free will?" wondered Sharon.

"Think of the opposite," suggested Mrs. Harris. "Like suppose you had a wind-up toy and whenever you wound it up it said, 'I love you, Sharon, I love you, Sharon,' over and over. There used to be little monkey toys like that. You'd wind one up, and it would jump around banging cymbals until it ran down. What would you think of a toy like that compared to the way Snickers loves you, for example?"

Snickers was there, of course. He could never resist a fire, but would probably have come for Sharon anyway. He was lying on the sheepskin rug with them, curled up against Sharon's stomach, but hearing his name, he looked up inquiringly at Mrs. Harris. She reached over and rumpled his ears.

"Yeah," Sharon thought this over. "You mean that if we didn't have free will, we would love God, but we wouldn't get to choose. We'd just automatically do it."

"Right," said Mrs. Harris. "So that's the beginning of the explanation. You see, somehow, it's worth it to God to give us free will, even though sometimes we do bad things. Then the second part of the explanation is that Adam and Eve used their free will to choose to disobey."

"That was in the catechism," said Sharon.

"So, you already know that it was their disobedience that brought death into the world? Am I going on too long? We could stop here until tomorrow," suggested Mrs. Harris, looking keenly at the little girl.

"No, no," responded Sharon. "This is really interesting. It's important stuff, isn't it?"

Mrs. Harris nodded. "The most important there is, really. Because the thing is that death wasn't meant to be. God didn't intend it when He made the world. And it's a terrible enemy. I know that Fr. Karimu's told you a couple of times what it took to conquer death."

Sharon was staring into the fire again, but she looked up at that. "It's why Jesus died."

"That's right," agreed Mrs. Harris. "Which is really the same as saying that God died, because Jesus really is God and really is a man too. 'For God so loved the world that he gave his only begotten Son, that whosoever believeth in him should not perish but have everlasting life,'" she quoted. "That's a version of the Bible with older English."

"I like it," said Sharon. "Believeth."

"Anyway, that's also really the best answer to your fears," she continued. "Jesus doesn't say that bad things won't happen. In fact, He says that they will, but not to be afraid because He has overcome the world, and He's always with us. Some of the times I've felt the closest to God have been when bad things happen, if I ask Him to help."

"Really?" Sharon was surprised.

"Really," affirmed Mrs. Harris.

"How does that work?" persisted Sharon.

"I told you once before," said Mrs. Harris. "Do you remember that talk we had a while back when you first began to believe in God, and I said that the times I've been in the most pain have also been the times I felt closest to God?"

"Yeah, I do. I wondered why you said that."

Mrs. Harris thought for a minute. "Well, one example is that once when I was in the hospital with pneumonia they needed to find out how much oxygen was in my blood. I was about thirty, I guess. A long time ago. These days they just clip a thing on your finger. It shines a light that goes through your finger and a machine tells them a number and it doesn't hurt at all, you don't even feel it, but in those days they had to stick a needle into my arm all the way down to an artery and take some blood out so they could do a test that they called 'arterial blood gases.'"

"Ooh, gross," Sharon shivered. "I hate needles."

"Yeah, I think everybody does," agreed Mrs. Harris. "Have you learned about veins and arteries in school, yet?"

Sharon nodded yes, then frowned with concentration. "We were just doing that. Arteries carry blood from your heart to the other parts of your body, and veins are what carry the blood back to your heart, right?"

"Right. But the thing is that usually if they test your blood they take blood from a vein, and it turns out that those are near the surface of your skin, but arteries are much farther down and deeper in." She gestured at her arm to show what she meant.

"Ouch!" exclaimed Sharon.

"Yes, 'ouch'! I've had a lot of physical pain in my life, but I really think that was the worst so far. But at the same time that it was hurting so much, I cried out to Jesus—in my mind, you know, not out loud—and I felt like He was holding me so close and suffering with me. I felt really comforted, like you did when you were so scared and God reached down to you."

She smiled at the memory. Sharon was sitting up in front of the fire now, hugging her knees, and she said, "That sounds really awful."

"It was really awful," admitted Mrs. Harris. "But the thing is that when I remember it, what I remember is feeling so close to Jesus. Another example isn't so bad." She smiled. "I'd had an operation, and they gave me morphine after it for the pain. Morphine is a really strong drug," she explained, "a painkiller, and I'd had it before, after other operations, but this time it did something really, really strange to me, and suddenly I couldn't swallow."

"Couldn't swallow?" asked Sharon. "Like what?"

"Like I'd need to swallow, but my body just wouldn't," answered Mrs. Harris. "You know, usually we don't think about swallowing. We just do it without paying attention. But you'd be surprised how often you need to swallow when you can't do it, and what a desperate feeling it is."

They both swallowed, then looked at each other and laughed.

"Yeah," said Mrs. Harris. "Just talking about it makes you want to swallow, doesn't it? Anyway, I called the nurse, and she gave me some apple juice to drink. It turned out that if I took a sip of apple juice or any other liquid, it would trigger my body to swallow automatically, but otherwise I just couldn't do it. It took about six hours for the morphine to wear off, even though they stopped it right away and gave me something else for pain."

Sharon looked up and shook her head sympathetically.

"But the point is," concluded Mrs. Harris, "that every time I took a sip of juice and swallowed, I'd say, 'Thank you, Jesus.' So now, when I look back on it, I mostly remember how grateful I was for this thing that we usually take completely for granted, and how close I felt to Jesus. Does that help you understand what I was talking about?"

Sharon nodded slowly. "Yeah, I guess. I want to try it." She thought for a little bit, then added, "But I don't want anything bad to happen to me just so I can."

Mrs. Harris chuckled. "Of course, not—nobody does. Enough bad things happen in life that you're bound to get a chance to try it out sooner or later. Sooner than you want to, I'm sure."

Sharon nodded again. Then she thought of something else.

"But you said that Jesus conquered death by dying for us, but then why does my daddy still have to die?" she asked. "I know I asked Fr. Karimu, but I don't really understand."

Mrs. Harris said, "Everybody still dies, but the death and rising to life again of Jesus are what opened the gates of heaven. Until then, they were closed. That's what Jesus was doing during the three days that He was in the grave: freeing people from hell and opening the gates of heaven so that after death we can be happy forever with God. Hell wasn't hell the way it is now. It was just a place where people had to wait after they died. The Bible calls it *Gehenna* or *Sheol*; it's kind of a holding place for the dead. Or it was.

"Besides that," she added, "I've often thought that God doesn't take death as seriously as we do. I mean," she went on, seeing the puzzled expression on the girl's face, "Jesus said that for God all people are alive, whether they're dead or alive.

"It's like this little story I once read," she went on, "almost a joke, really, about twins who weren't born yet—they were still inside their mother's tummy," she put it in child language. "And they were having a discussion about whether there was life after birth!"

Sharon laughed, "Life after *birth*?"

"Yes, life after birth," Mrs. Harris confirmed, and laughed, too. "One of them thought there wasn't, that birth was the end of everything, but the other twin was more hopeful and thought that there might be something—some other kind of life—after you were born."

"That's kind of like us, isn't it?" asked Sharon. "I mean, here we are, sitting and talking about is there life after death."

"Probably just as silly," agreed Mrs. Harris, then looked at her watch.

"My goodness, I've kept you too late. You'd better apologize to your mother for me, please."

They stood up, and Sharon gave Mrs. Harris a big hug. She couldn't say anything, but Mrs. Harris knew she was grateful and patted her on the back, then escorted her to the front door and watched her run home.

Chapter 20

In the Night

Time passed. Mrs. Harris and Sharon finished *When Hitler Stole Pink Rabbit* and were deeply into *A Little Princess* by Frances Hodgson Burnett. Sharon was loving the story. Now that Sara was poor, she had started getting help from the Indian gentleman who had moved in next door, though she didn't yet know who it was who had transformed her attic room. The Tasha Tudor illustrations made the book even better, and Sharon loved the fact that they were reading the very copy of the book that Mrs. Harris had been given for her tenth birthday. There was a bookplate inside the front cover with the name "Wilma" written in childish cursive.

It was still Lent, but Holy Week was coming soon.

There came a night in early April when Sharon was woken up abruptly after she had been asleep for some hours. Her mother turned on the light in Sharon's bedroom and called to her. There was something in her mother's voice that jolted Sharon out of her sound sleep and made her fight her way back to full consciousness quickly.

"Get up!" Sharon's mother said "Sharon, you've got to get up."

"Why?" asked Sharon.

"The hospital called," her mother explained. "They said we've got to come right away."

Sharon climbed out of bed and dressed as quickly as she could. The clock on her table said 3:15. That wasn't a time she'd ever been awake before. She felt disoriented by the bright room light which hurt her sleep-filled eyes. Her hands shook as she tried to do up the buttons on a sweater. She tried to think but was full of dread. "Jesus?" she tried a tentative prayer. "Please help!"

When her mother came down the hallway again to see if Sharon was dressed, Sharon asked her, "Mama, is Daddy dying?"

Her mother's face looked white and strained. There were dark circles under her eyes. She looked at Sharon in a troubled way, and her voice shook as she answered, "I think so. They said we'd better come if we wanted to say good-bye."

"Mama, we've got to call Fr. Karimu," said Sharon urgently, following her mother's quick steps down the hallway.

"Oh, Sharon, there's no time for that," her mother said impatiently.

"It's important," Sharon insisted. "Daddy would want us to."

Her mother was almost beside herself. "Sharon, honey, we don't have *time* for this!"

"Mama, *please*," Sharon pleaded. "We've gotta have time for it. It's *important*," she said again.

"Well, then, you'll have to call him yourself," her mother declared. "I'm not going to call any priest at three AM. What a waste of time when we're supposed to be hurrying!"

She went on talking to herself, complaining, but Sharon had streaked back to her room where she knew she had the card with Fr. Karimu's phone number on it, which Mrs. Harris had given her at Christmas. Although she was scared to bother the priest in the middle of the night, she just took a deep breath and didn't give herself time to think. She heard the phone ring five or six times after she dialed, then a sleepy voice said, "Hello," and she recognized the deep voice and Tanzanian accent of Fr. Karimu.

"Father, it's me, Sharon," she said breathlessly. "My daddy's dying. The hospital called and told us and we're leaving now and can you come?" Her words all ran together.

Fr. Karimu replied, "I will come, Sharon. Don't worry. I will see you there."

Sharon and her mother went out to the car. The night was chilly, and Sharon shivered, in spite of her coat, until the heater got going. She noticed that her mother was shaking, too, and wondered if maybe she was too upset to drive, but there wasn't anything she could do about it.

When they got to the hospital, she followed her mother across the parking lot. Their steps sounded loud on the asphalt pavement. She was glad to step into the warm brightness of the Emergency Room, which seemed to be the only entrance open in the middle of the night.

Entering the building through this different door left Sharon disoriented. She followed her mother down the shining, immaculately clean corridors with arrows and signs pointing to places with names that Sharon had never heard of. What was "Nephrology," she wondered.

Sharon's mom walked quickly, not at all confused by having had to come in a different way. Sharon had to trot to keep up. They went through a double set of swinging doors, labeled "Oncology, Rms 201-254," then stopped at a doorway about halfway down on the right. This was the other side of the hall from what Sharon was used to, but she saw the familiar paper label saying "Stover" in black magic marker. This was her father's room.

Sharon peered inside and saw a strange scene. The room was about half lit. It contained the bed with her father in it, as usual, but at first she didn't recognize him, because there seemed to be tubes all over him, connected to various machines or bottles that were now standing near the bed.

Also standing near the head of the bed was Fr. Karimu, taking off the stole he had been wearing. Apparently, he had just heard Mr. Stover's confession. The Cathedral, where he lived in one of the houses on the quadrangle, was not far from the VA Hospital. Clearly, he had beaten them there by quite a while. Sharon and her mother crept up to the bed, and Sharon began to recognize bits of her father among all the tubes. His eyes, for example, were recognizable, and one hand was on the blanket covering him.

She couldn't bring herself to kiss him but went forward and took his hand. His skin was a strange white color that she had never seen before, and he seemed to be fighting for breath. He spoke in little gasps, half a sentence at a time.

Sharon looked at him and tears came to her eyes which she tried to blink away.

"Oh, Daddy," was all she could find to say.

Fr. Karimu stood by her and took her free hand in his warm one, in noticeable contrast to the cold hand of her father. She leaned against him, and he changed hands, putting his other arm around her shoulders.

Her father made an effort and smiled at her, then said, "Sharon, I wanted to see you. I wanted to tell you ... Sharon, don't be afraid, Honey... I'm not afraid any more..."

"I'm trying not to be, Daddy." Sharon was crying. "Mrs. Harris is helping and, Daddy, I do believe in God now."

"That's right," he nodded, then added, "Remember to go to Mass ... That's important ... Always remember that."

"I will, Daddy. And I'll pray for you, Daddy, but I wish you didn't have to go away."

"Me, too..." His eyes closed for a moment, while he gathered strength from somewhere. Then he said, "Remember this ... Someone said ... 'Christians never have to say good-bye.'"

Sharon found the courage to kiss him on the cheek, then she was sent out to sit on her usual bench in the hallway while her dad spoke with her mother. After a minute or two, Fr. Karimu joined Sharon on the bench, looking tired but comfortably solid and beautifully brown in contrast to the wraithlike thinness and strange pallor of her own father.

He smiled tenderly at Sharon as he sat down on the bench beside her, taking her hand again. Again, Sharon leaned against him, shut her eyes, and just rested for a minute or two.

Then, Fr. Karimu spoke to her, saying, "In a few minutes I am going to anoint your father and give him last rites. Would you like to watch? It would be good, I think."

Sharon thought for a moment, wondering if she had the courage to go back into that room and see her father lying there hooked up to all those machines again. Then she nodded.

"Why's he so white?" she whispered.

"It's something that happens before people die," Fr. Karimu said softly. "It's called the death pallor, but that just means whiteness, like what you saw."

Sharon nodded, but didn't speak.

They waited a few more minutes until Sharon's mother opened the door to her husband's room. Her eyes were red, and her face flushed, but otherwise she seemed to have herself under control. "He's ready," she said.

Fr. Karimu and Sharon got up and walked back into the room, Fr. Karimu putting on his stole again as he walked. Sharon's mother stayed near the door and watched while Fr. Karimu went over to a small black leather case he had left on the nightstand next to the bed. He took from it a white cloth, the size of a pocket handkerchief, which he laid carefully on the tray table. Then he took a small gold case from his shirt pocket, a black book from his jacket pocket and started, "In the name of the Father, and of the Son, and of the Holy Spirit…" Sharon crossed herself, watching her father. His eyes had been closed, but they opened now, and he moved his hand in the best approximation he could make to the sign of the cross.

The beauty of the prayers resonated deeply within Sharon, and she drew comfort from watching the quiet competence with which Fr. Karimu went about what he was doing.

Sharon's father seemed almost beyond speech now, but he managed to say "Amen" before Fr. Karimu put the fragment of Host on his tongue. His breathing had become unsteady. He would take several breaths in a row, then miss a breath or two, resume breathing, then miss again.

Sharon found herself listening to the increasing pauses between breaths. All three of them stood silent, watching this fight for breath. A nurse came in and walked quickly to the bed, taking the dying man's wrist in her hand and feeling for the pulse at his neck. She looked at the watchers and shook her head slightly. "He's going," she mouthed.

Then, Sharon saw something beautiful happen. Her father's eyes lit up and he smiled, as though he was seeing something. This coincided with what turned out to be his last breath. A loud, continuous beep filled the room as they listened in vain for the sound of the next breath. It didn't come. The nurse put down his hand, moved to shut the now-unseeing eyes, and said to them, "I'm afraid he's gone." She busied herself turning off the machine that was making noise, then shut the valves on the IV.

Sharon had never seen the dead body of a person. It shocked her to see her father lying so still. She watched while the adults talked above her head, wondering if she would see *some* movement, but there wasn't any. Her father's body lay completely inert, still with a smile about his lips.

She turned to Fr. Karimu, who looked down at her. He saw a certain forlornness in her expression, which she knew nothing of, but which led him to pick her up off the ground and hold her close for a long minute.

The embrace seemed healing somehow; she could feel the beating of the priest's heart and her own and was suddenly aware that *they* still belonged to life. He put her down, and she turned to her mother, putting out her arms. Her mother grabbed her and hugged her tightly. Tears ran down both of their faces as they stood for a long minute, locked in each other's arms. Finally, her mother released her. Sharon turned again to the bed, looking at her father's body.

She had heard people talk about the body being an empty shell after death, that the person wasn't really there any more. But where was he? If he wasn't in his body, and she could see that he wasn't, he must be somewhere. She could still summon up his personality in her mind, and it came to her strongly that death couldn't be the end. Her father must be somewhere. On the other hand, and at the same time, it also looked to her as though her father might wake up any minute. But the minutes passed while the grownups talked, making some kind of arrangements. She didn't listen to the talk, just looked at her father's body. It didn't move. She was beginning to realize that he really was gone.

Finally, the nurse pulled a sheet over the body. That made it almost more frightening to Sharon, and she was glad to leave the room so she could stop watching the sheet to make sure it didn't move even a little bit.

Sharon's mom looked down at her once they were in the hallway and said tiredly. "We can go home now, Honey, at least until morning, later in the morning I should say. Then I'll have to do some more arranging."

Fr. Karimu walked them out to their car. Sharon's mother managed to rise to the occasion and thank him for coming. "I know it meant a lot to my husband," she said.

Sharon, herself, looked into his eyes for a moment, trying to put into her look how grateful she was. He put his arms around her shoulders, and she hugged him around the waist for a moment, then she climbed into the car.

The sun wasn't up yet, but the sky was beginning to lighten as they drove along. Sharon was surprised to see that everything had transpired in only three hours. It was just after 6:30 in the morning and traffic was beginning to build for the morning rush hour.

Sharon's mother drove home, then suggested that they eat a little something and go back to bed. She told Sharon that she'd make some phone calls but that she wouldn't go to work that day, and Sharon wouldn't go to school, probably, for the rest of the week.

After a scant breakfast of toast and orange juice, Sharon was sent back to bed to try to catch up on her sleep. As she put her pajamas back on and climbed under the covers, she wondered if she would be able to sleep. Tears seemed far from her at that moment. So much had happened in the night that she was overwhelmed by it. In fact, rather than crying or lying awake mulling over the events of the last hours she fell asleep right away—a respite from grief.

She woke up in time for lunch, then headed over to Mrs. Harris's house. Her mother was glad that Sharon had something better to do than accompany her to the funeral parlor where decisions needed to be made but asked for a quick phone call from Mrs. Harris to verify that Sharon was welcome so early.

Sharon rang Mrs. Harris's doorbell, heard the usual commotion as Snickers tore back and forth between the front door and Mrs. Harris, barking wildly. When Mrs. Harris came to the door, she immediately took in the meaning of Sharon's being there so early and a look of pain crossed her face.

"Oh, no," she said, as she opened the door and let Sharon in.

Snickers danced around, welcoming her now, but no less noisy, and Sharon had to bend down and pat him before he was willing to settle down so that Sharon and Mrs. Harris could make themselves heard. "It's bad news, isn't it?" asked Mrs. Harris at last. "I heard your car in the middle of the night."

"Yes," said Sharon, "Daddy died. Could you call my mom if it's okay for me to be here this early? She wants to go to the funeral home, but she'll take me, too, if it's inconvenient for me to be here so early." She was parroting what her mother had said.

Sharon was welcome, and Mrs. Harris made the phone call right away. Sharon listened as Mrs. Harris told her mother that she knew there were a lot of things that needed to be done when someone died, and that she'd be happy to watch Sharon anytime Mrs. Stover needed her to. "This week isn't very full for me," she ended.

When she hung up, Sharon asked, "You weren't at home when we got back from the hospital, were you? Your car was gone. I was thinking I'd come tell you if I saw your lights on."

Mrs. Harris explained that she must already have left for swimming at the Y. Sharon knew that Mrs. Harris swam every morning then went to daily Mass at a nearby church, but she somehow hadn't realized that it all started so early.

"Tell me about it now," suggested Mrs. Harris, and Sharon told her everything she could remember about the previous night's events. Mrs. Harris commented on Sharon's having the courage to call Fr. Karimu at three o'clock in the morning, but Sharon made light of it, now that it was over, just saying that she knew she had to.

The rest of the story moved Mrs. Harris to tears more than once. When she heard about, "Christians never have to say good-bye," she remarked that it was C. S. Lewis, author of the Narnia books, who had said that to a friend.

Sharon told Mrs. Harris how her father had smiled at the end, just before he died.

"I've heard of that," said Mrs. Harris. "Somebody called it being 'radiant in death,' I think."

When Sharon had told her everything, Mrs. Harris shook her head and sighed.

"It was a good death, wasn't it?" was her only comment.

Sharon said, "Fr. Karimu was so nice! You know, it's like that's what he's for. I mean, he just seemed to know what he was doing, and he was so calm and really comforting."

"He's a good priest," Mrs. Harris remarked. "And you're right. Priests see a lot of deaths, compared to the rest of us. It's part of their job, shepherding people who are dying."

For the rest of the week, Sharon spent more time than usual with Mrs. Harris. They had a pretty good three days, talking about things, finishing off *A Little Princess* and starting another Frances Hodgson Burnett book, *The Secret Garden*, which again had belonged to Mrs. Harris in childhood. This one grabbed Sharon from the very first sentence.

The funeral was on Friday and was the first one Sharon had ever attended. She almost didn't get to go. Mrs. Stover considered her to be too young, but after a struggle and consultation with Fr. Karimu and Mrs. Harris, Sharon was allowed to take part.

The funeral was held at the Cathedral. A lot of her father's colleagues from work attended, as well as a few out-of-town relatives.

Sharon's mother was an only child. Her father had two sisters, but his parents had preceded him in death. While her mother's mother was still alive, she was in a nursing home and couldn't travel to come to a funeral. So, there weren't very many close relatives, though Sharon's aunts both came.

Sharon found the funeral difficult but was glad she had gone. Some of the prayers were comforting to her, but she had trouble realizing that her father's body was really in the box that was sitting at the front of the church, draped with a United States flag because her father had been a veteran.

Two days after the funeral, Sharon went to Mass with Mrs. Harris. Sharon and Mrs. Harris had a talk about what might await her at school on Monday. Sharon knew that the other children might "act weird" around her, as she put it. She really didn't want to go back to school. Mrs. Harris agreed that the children wouldn't know how to treat Sharon, but pointed out that she'd have to go through the same thing whenever she went back and thought that she might as well get it over with. Delay wouldn't really help.

Monday came, and Mrs. Harris went to school to get Sharon as always, expecting to hear a report about how the day had gone. She wasn't disappointed. Sharon told her that it had pretty much fulfilled her worst expectations. Most of the children hadn't known what to say and had contented themselves with just looking at her, "with weird expressions," as Sharon put it. Two or three teachers had come up and gushed all over her about how sorry they were, wanting to hug her and succeeding only in embarrassing her half to death.

Mrs. Harris pointed out that the worst was now over and re-marked that people have short memories for other people's trage-dies. This proved to be true. Things at school were soon back to nor-mal.

Sharon and Mrs. Harris talked about her father's death some-times. Sharon missed her father of course, but, in a sense, she had already been missing him for months as he had gotten sicker and sicker. And her dominant impression of his death was that it hadn't been "that scary," as she put it. She was especially struck by how he had smiled at the end.

"People say that when you're dying you sometimes see people you know who have already died," Mrs. Harris told Sharon. "People like your mother and father, maybe, or a grandmother, a friend. It depends. And I've heard of people seeing angels. We don't really know, do we?"

Chapter 21

October Again

Six months later, on a Sunday night in October, Mrs. Harris was having a party to celebrate Sharon's tenth birthday and the first anniversary of their meeting.

Sharon and her mother were there as well as Fr. Karimu. Everyone was sitting around the kitchen table, full of the pizza they had just enjoyed. The women were sipping juice or cider. Fr. Karimu was making himself a cup of tea, using hot water from the thermos that Mrs. Harris always set out for him. Now, he stirred sugar into his cup: one, two, three, four spoonfuls.

Sharon was inured to this by now and didn't notice what he was doing until she saw her mother's eyes widen with surprise. She smiled at her mother and their eyes twinkled at each other, but they didn't say anything.

Mrs. Harris, too, caught the byplay and smiled. "It's typically African," she murmured to Mrs. Stover.

"What is?" asked Fr. Karimu.

"Putting so much sugar in a cup of tea," answered Mrs. Harris. "I think it surprises Americans that a small cup of tea can even dissolve that much sugar. I don't think, besides Africans, that I ever saw anybody put more than two spoonfuls of sugar into a teacup."

Fr. Karimu was unruffled. "Very sweet, very good," was his only comment.

Are people ready for birthday cake?" asked Mrs. Harris. She stood up and fetched a magnificent white-frosted cake decorated with rosebuds and ten pink candles, which had been reposing on the kitchen counter. There were two kinds of ice cream—strawberry and vanilla. Mrs. Harris lit the ten candles, then they all sang "Happy Birthday" to an embarrassed Sharon who blushed pinker than the candles.

"There is nothing so good as this in my country," said Fr. Karimu, once Sharon had made a silent wish, blown out the candles (on her first try), and the cake was served to him.

"*Mtori*?" questioned Mrs. Harris.

"Oh, well maybe *mtori*," he agreed.

"What is that?" asked Mrs. Stover.

"It's the most wonderful soup, made from green bananas with a little onion. It's the staple food of Father's tribe, the Chaggas. Do you remember when the Superior General's brother was in the hospital with pneumonia? A kitchen worker took him a thermos of *mtori* every day, and it kept him alive. We used to say in Tanzania that it was too good for the First World," Mrs. Harris reminisced.

"I remember," said Fr. Karimu, laughing out loud.

Presents were eminently satisfactory. Fr. Karimu took a small package, wrapped in white paper, from the pocket of his jacket and handed it to Sharon. When she opened it, she saw a little giraffe, carved from wood and painted.

"A giraffe!" she exclaimed.

"It's a *twiga*," Fr. Karimu said. He pronounced it "twee-gah." "I thought of you this summer when I was at home in Tanzania. I thought you might like it."

"*Twiga* is the Swahili word for giraffe," put in Mrs. Harris. "I always used to say that it was my favorite Swahili word."

"It's really neat," Sharon said as she hefted it in her hand. "Thank you, Father."

"Happy birthday," he rejoined.

Mrs. Stover mentioned that she had a few presents at home for Sharon, notably some much-needed pajamas, but also handed her daughter a birthday card. Sharon had to study it for a minute to get the meaning. "Does this say I can have something new for my nativity set?" she asked at last.

"That's right," smiled her mother. "Maybe not the biggest, most expensive thing, but we'll find something. Mrs. Harris said she can tell us where to shop."

"Gee," Sharon's eyes grew dreamy. "I could maybe get an ox, or a Wise Man, or at least a sheep. Thank you, Mama."

Mrs. Harris handed over her present. It was rectangular, not very heavy, and proved to be two pictures in light wooden frames. One was of Jesus standing, arm raised, at a door in what looked like a garden. He seemed to be listening intently. Apparently, He had just knocked on the door. The other picture showed a beautiful big lady with wings, walking behind a little boy and girl as they crossed a footbridge over a roiling river.

"That's a guardian angel," commented Mrs. Harris.

"I think I've seen the other one before," Mrs. Stover said. "I almost think maybe I had one when I was little. My grandmother might have given it to me. She was a devout Christian."

"They're both very famous pictures and they've been around for a long time," said Mrs. Harris. "I can help you hang them, Sharon, if you need help."

"Oh, I think we can manage it," responded Mrs. Stover. "I'm not exactly handy—Jim always did those things—but we've got finishing nails and the pictures aren't heavy. Maybe above your bed?" she asked Sharon.

"Maybe. Let's look later and decide," answered Sharon. "Thank you, Mrs. Harris. They're great." Suddenly, a thought struck her. "Snickers should have a treat on my birthday."

"A dog biscuit?" asked Mrs. Harris.

"No, a real treat," pleaded Sharon. "Cake or ice cream or something."

"Those wouldn't be good for him," answered Mrs. Harris. "I'll tell you what we might do, though," she added, studying the pizza plates which had been put on the counter next to the kitchen sink. "He loves pizza crusts, and I rarely give him any. Look," she said to Sharon, "isn't that a big piece of crust that you didn't eat? It's even got a little tomato sauce on it. You may give him that if you like. He'll love it, and it will take him quite a while to eat it, too."

Sharon got up and walked over to the counter. She looked at her plate. "Yes," she agreed, picking up the rather large piece of crust. Snickers was dancing around hoping it was for him. Sharon made the usual hand gesture as she told him to sit. Then she reached down with the crust. He took it delicately between his jaws and walked over to the edge of the hall carpeting with it. He was so pleased that he couldn't help frisking a little.

"It's been quite a year for you," Mrs. Harris commented to Sharon as she resumed her seat at the table. "Think of all that's happened."

"Daddy died, that's the big thing," answered Sharon. "I really miss him."

"You'll always miss him," said Mrs. Harris. "I miss all my relatives and friends who have died."

"But at the same time, it was so un-scary," said Sharon. "He looked so peaceful. And the way he smiled at the end. I don't know what I expected, but I didn't expect that."

"It was a beautiful death," Fr. Karimu said. "Beautiful because it was a prepared death, and he accepted it. I see many people die and it is not always so nice. But, of course, it is hard for you and your mother. Grieving takes a long time, and you will always miss him."

Sharon's mother nodded agreement, but didn't seem able to speak.

"Six months already, isn't it?" asked Mrs. Harris.

"That is true," said Fr. Karimu. "It was April and now it is October."

"And I met Mrs. Harris and started learning about Jesus and the Church, and then I met you, Father, and all the reading and everything. And I'm in the fifth grade now." Sharon ran out of words.

"You are at the beginning of your journey to God," pointed out Fr. Karimu. "There are many, many things to know—much to learn," he finished.

"Have you noticed that you don't shake anymore?" asked Mrs. Harris. "I just thought of that. And you don't jump in that startled way you used to have when there was a sudden noise."

"That's true," agreed Mrs. Stover. "I haven't seen you do that for a long time, Sharon."

"I don't know why," mused Sharon. "Nothing really changed, but everything changed. It's confusing."

"You learned how to pray," suggested Mrs. Harris. "You know where to turn for help now."

Sharon nodded.

"And you've grown up some," suggested Sharon's mother. "Look at how you keep your room clean and even help me with the living room. You're not just a little girl anymore."

"You are surrounded by people who love you: your mother, Mrs. Harris, me," added Fr. Karimu. "We would all help."

"You do all help." Sharon smiled at them.

"Let's make cheers," proposed Fr. Karimu, only he pronounced it "chee-yahs."

"What's that?" asked Sharon.

Fr. Karimu smiled. "That is a custom of my country," he said.

"Cheers," Mrs. Harris pronounced it in the American way. "Actually, I think you got it from the British."

"Probably," he agreed. "We got many things, both good and bad, from them."

"I think we'd say 'toast,'" said Mrs. Harris. "You need your drink to do it. Anyone need a refill?"

After glasses had been topped up, Mrs. Harris took the lead. "Like this," she said as she raised her glass.

"First we must stand up," said Fr. Karimu.

"That's right," admitted Mrs. Harris.

They all stood up.

Mrs Harris raised her glass again. "To friendship! she said. "Now you touch everyone's glass gently, with your glass." She illustrated, touching Mrs. Stover's glass with hers. Fr. Karimu reached across the table to touch glasses with each of the women and Sharon.

When they all had touched glasses, Mrs. Harris said, "Now take a sip of your drink. But be sure to save some for the next toast. That's how you make 'chee-yahs.'"

"To reading!" Sharon lifted her glass. She touched Mrs. Harris's glass, then her mother's, then Fr. Karimu's. The adults all touched glasses, too. Everyone took a sip of drink.

"To lovingkindness!" proposed Mrs. Stover, looking at Mrs. Harris as she spoke.

"To Sharon on her tenth birthday!" finished Fr. Karimu when it was his turn. They touched glasses one last time then drained them on this last toast.

"Well, now we start the second year of our friendship," Mrs. Harris smiled at Sharon.

"So … what are we going to read next?" asked Sharon, her eyes shining.

The Books They Read

Berenstain, Stan, and Jan Berenstain. *The Berenstain Bears and the Messy Room.* Random House, 1983.

Berry, Joy Wilt. *What To Do When Your Mom or Dad Says, "Clean Up Your Room."* Children's Press, 1981.

Braenne, Berit. *Trina Finds a Brother.* Translated by Evelyn Ramsden, William Morrow, 1960.

Burnett, Frances Hodgson. *A Little Princess.* Charles Scribner's Sons, 1905.

---. *The Secret Garden.* Frederick A. Stokes Company, 1911.

Canfield, Dorothy. *Understood Betsy.* Henry Holt and Company, 1916.

De Angeli, Marguerite. *The Lion in the Box.* Doubleday, 1975.

Gates, Doris. *A Morgan for Melinda.* Viking Press, 1961.

Godden, Rumer. *Miss Happiness and Miss Flower.* Viking Press, 1961.

---. *The Kitchen Madonna.* Viking Press, 1967.

Kerr, Judith. *When Hitler Stole Pink Rabbit.* Collins, 1971.

Lewis, C. S. *The Chronicles of Narnia.* HarperCollins, 1950–1956.

- *The Lion, the Witch and the Wardrobe.* 1950.
- *Prince Caspian.* 1951.
- *The Voyage of the Dawn Treader.* 1952.
- *The Silver Chair.* 1953.
- *The Horse and His Boy.* 1954.
- *The Magician's Nephew.* 1955.
- *The Last Battle.* 1956.

MacDonald, Betty. *Nancy and Plum.* Lippincott, 1952.

Mason, Miriam E. *Matilda and Her Family.* Bobbs-Merrill, 1948.

Morris, Ruth. *Runaway Girl.* E. P. Dutton, 1961.

Potter, Beatrix. *The Tale of Benjamin Bunny.* Frederick Warne & Co., 1904.

Warner, Gertrude Chandler. *The Boxcar Children.* Rand McNally, 1942.

www.ingramcontent.com/pod-product-compliance
Lightning Source LLC
Chambersburg PA
CBHW011717240626
47153CB00009B/2900